Chronopticus Rising
Book III of the Chronopticus Chronicles

By Michael Galloway

ISBN-13: 978-0-9847402-7-7

www.michaelgalloway.net

This is a work of fiction. Names, characters, places, and events are products of the author's imagination or are used fictitiously. Any resemblance to actual persons, living or dead, locations, or events is entirely coincidental.

All Scripture verses taken from the King James Version of the Bible.

Chapter One
Winter 2060 A.D.
Under the Magnopolis Dome, Mars

When Pierce Steadman awoke he realized that not only was he no longer the mayor of Magnopolis, but that everything he worked for over the past few months was now in the hands of a madman. As he sat up, his notebook of architectural dreams tumbled out of his lap and onto the floor. He overheard his girlfriend, Suzanne Entner, and her sister, Lisabeth, having an animated discussion in the living room. The prior week's events left him in a state of bewilderment: Ionotatron had fallen into a heap in the Martian desert, Suzanne had been rescued from the Chronopticus prison, and he was supposed to believe some great rebellion was still threatening the city.

As the minutes wore on, the idea of an ongoing rebellion faded from his mind. It was replaced by the thought that he had been played as a fool by the leadership of the Dexler Corporation and left to blame for the destruction of the city. He did not have the mindset or the patience to look into the legalities of his removal from office and so he stood up and took a deep breath.

He wandered out to the living room to the sounds of news reports on the wall telescreen. All the while his mind kept replaying the speech from the night before by the CEO of the Dexler Corporation, Kalen Rusk. Thoughts of Kalen having broad, sweeping, emergency powers until the rebellion ended made him wonder if it was nothing more than a power grab. As he ran a hand through his hair, his eyes attempted to focus on the screen.

A female news reporter with long, straight, silver-blonde hair and a raspy voice stood in the middle of downtown, with the City Center building in the background. She pointed to the lines behind her that stretched around the block, and although her lips were moving, he closed his ears to her words. His weary eyes drifted to the bottom of the screen. A scrolling headline read: "Kalen Rusk, CEO of Dexler Corporation, takes control of city. Pierce Steadman, former mayor, steps down."

He turned to Suzanne. "I didn't step down. I was thrown out." He stared on at her black, shoulder-length hair and then at her hazel eyes. Although she was half-Romanian and half-English, the look in her eyes was all business as if her mind focused on a distant goal.

"We need to go pick up our food badges," she said with a frown. She stood up from the sofa. They had spent the night at Lisabeth's house and Pierce wondered what type of crowd they would face this morning on the streets. James, Suzanne's son, stood by her side, as Lisabeth rose up from the sofa, too.

"I wonder what's in the badges," Pierce muttered.

"What do you mean?"

"I doubt they're just pieces of plastic. They probably have a tracking device in them. At a minimum."

The more Pierce thought about it, the more he wondered if he even wanted the badges stored anywhere inside their houses. Perhaps they could drop them off in a hidden box just outside the door or only use them when they needed to shop at the market. He was familiar with the City Council plans to implement the badge system in case of an emergency. He had even handled one before and his intuition told him they were capable of vast amounts of data collection. The badges were meant to be temporary, but something told him Kalen planned on taking full advantage of this opportunity to add to his data collection system, even if that meant implementing the badges on a permanent basis.

The four of them walked to the front door and out into the street. The Cyclodes Pierce noted prowling the neighborhood the night before were gone except for the one that stood still on the corner of Julia Street and Edison Avenue near the city Coliseum. It was a model that he and Omar Goldman modified in order to take on Ionotatron, but it appeared to have been repurposed for enforcement.

As they walked toward the City Center, Pierce could hear a loudspeaker being used by city officials or law enforcement. As they passed the Coliseum, with its circular array of alternating arches and pillars, the words from the loudspeaker became distinct, if not repetitive. The voice sounded mechanical, rather than human, and it was at that moment he recalled how Omar's experiments with speech synthesis were incorporated into the Sentinels' most recent upgrades.

"Please divide yourselves into two lines. Once you receive your badge, please exit the area quickly. All badges must be worn in public at all times and need to be presented when requested by the authorities," said the mechanical voice.

They then passed the soon-to-open Towers of Venice Casino, with its three rebuilt floors, real canals full of artificially-rippled water, and Renaissance-era feel to its architecture. Pierce could only imagine the opulence inside.

He looked around at the street curbs and noticed tiny, round, black bumps at regular intervals on their surfaces. Then he glanced up at a streetlamp as they passed underneath it. Why he never paid attention to such details before he never knew.

"What is it?" Suzanne said as she tightened the grip on his hand.

He leaned over and whispered into her ear. "I never noticed it before. It looks like there are data collection points embedded everywhere in the city. In the curbs, in the streetlights, and now on us."

Although she did not reply, he knew what she thought. He tightened his grip on James' hand. Their pace slowed as if none of them wanted to face the reception line for badges.

The four of them turned onto Pascal Avenue and then walked toward the City Center building. It was the tallest building in Magnopolis, and at seven stories high, it left little room between its top and the underside of the dome that protected the city from the frigid, carbon-dioxide-filled Martian air outside. As they approached, a crew of construction workers hoisted a giant, round, analog clock into place on the side of the building. The clock face was pale blue and its slender black hands pointed straight up.

On the streets below, lines ran the length of the block as crowds waited to receive their badges. As citizens passed them by, Pierce studied their badges and noticed they radiated different colors. Some glowed yellow, but most were pearly white. Others were orange and a few were a crimson color. Several citizens stared at the badges, too, and all were attached on the right-hand side of their coats, shirts, or sweaters. All of the badges were an inch in diameter and shaped like a round shirt button.

"What do you think the colors mean?" He said to Suzanne.

"Maybe it determines how much food you can get."

"Or maybe it's a sorting system."

Up ahead of them, four older model Cyclode Sentinel machines stood guard over the lines, with two machines on each side, spaced several feet apart from each other. Each machine was six feet tall, blue and silver in color, and had a small, rectangular metal head with hydraulic-controlled arms and legs. The machines repeated the same phrases over and over every two minutes and quickly reached the point of monotony.

As they reached the back of one of the queue lines, Pierce scanned around at the faces and recognized some of the citizens. In the front of the line, he watched as Ruelle Dorner, her husband Ryan, and their daughter Jessie picked up their badges. At first, he thought that it was only one badge per household, which was the original plan as listed in the City Council office. Yet all three of them received a badge as well as verbal instructions on how to display them, when they were needed, and their purpose. As the three of them left the front of the line, he got a glimpse of their badge colors and in that moment, the system made sense.

"They just received orange badges," Pierce whispered to Suzanne.

"Meaning what?"

"Meaning they're being tagged. In the original system, the colors were supposed to represent what neighborhood you lived in. The badges were pretty basic and really nothing more than colored pieces of plastic with a simple chip inside. These look different. Same concept but a totally different design. And the colors. I think I know what red means."

Suzanne gave him a worried look.

He pressed on. "Kalen's sorting out the potential troublemakers."

"What makes you think that?"

"Ruelle helped bring down several of the Cyclode machines a few years ago when they started attacking people. But wait. Now that I think about it, her and her husband are regulars over at the city church. Unless..."

"Unless what?" She watched his eyes intently.

"Unless he's sorting out Christians."

As they passed the first set of Cyclode Sentinel machines on either side of the two queue lines, Pierce grew tired of the mechanical instructions being given out. "Please divide yourselves into two lines. Once you receive your badge please exit the area quickly. All badges must be worn in public at all times and need to be presented when requested by the authorities," said the voice again.

When they reached the front of the line, they stepped forward toward a makeshift stand where Arielle Warzecha, a City Council member, handed out badges. She gave them a brief smile and then checked her handheld video plate for their names. A black, rectangular machine next to her ejected the badges one by one. Pierce studied their colors.

"Are you still on the Council?" He asked as she handed him a badge.

"Yes," she said as she moved to the side and reached out to the next person in line behind him.

He felt himself being tugged along by an equally irritated Suzanne. He pulled back but was now being pushed aside by the family that stood behind them in line. He jumped up in an attempt to get Arielle's attention again.

"What color is your badge? Or don't you get one like the rest of us?"

"Pierce," Suzanne said. She yanked on his shirt sleeve with more force this time, nearly tearing it off.

He wanted to ask Arielle a thousand questions, but the pace of the line made that impossible. If she was still on the City Council, was she still in charge of the Accounting, Legal, and Human Resources departments for the city? If so, why was she still on the Council while he was taking the fall for all that went wrong as of late? The sight of her face annoyed him and he felt his pulse accelerate. If anyone should get a chance to make things right in the city it should be him, not her and the others on the Council.

He noted that Lisabeth and James each received white badges, while Suzanne's badge was a pale yellow color. His badge was the same shade of yellow. Arielle said nothing else to Pierce and pretended to ignore his departure.

As Pierce walked along, he turned the badge over in his hands and found no markings on it other than the words "Property of Dexler Corporation" in small print and a corporate logo on the back. "They make it look like you're an employee of theirs. Guess they need to check their records better."

Suzanne attached the badge to her shirt, but said nothing.

Meanwhile, he tried to make sense of it all. "So let me get this right. We took out Io, saved the city from attack, and then this?"

"I don't think this will continue forever."

He wanted to believe her. He really did. In defiance, he stuffed his badge out of sight and into his pants pocket. Another citizen passed by with a rose-colored badge.

"I'm hungry," James said as he looked toward the grocery store.

Pierce put on his best smile. "Me, too. But let's go home to eat, okay?" He looked back over to Suzanne and then down at her hand. For weeks, he wanted to buy her an engagement ring. Yet tonight he felt their future was slipping away faster than ever and that he needed to do something about it.

Chapter Two

After dinner at Suzanne's house, Pierce stopped by Gray's Clock and Jewelry Store. It was a small shop on the edge of downtown, across from the Public Works laboratory where Omar retrofitted several Cyclodes with a spherical spider weapon for use against Io. The store only had one window in the front and inside Artelius Gray stared out as if he dreamt of a vacation to a distant place.

Inside, the store was a mixture of jewelry displays, children's games, watches, and exotic clocks which hung on the walls. Artelius designed and built all of the watches and clocks himself. Each handcrafted timepiece appeared to a visitor from Earth to function just like an Earthly clock, yet the real difference was in the greater length of the Martian second due to the Martian day being several minutes longer. Pierce remembered how when he first moved here, time appeared to move slower, but it was only an illusion.

Artelius returned to stand behind the front counter. The jeweler was in his late sixties with thick glasses and wiry gray hair that was balding on top. His denim shirt and pants were time-worn and speckled with flecks of gold dust. His weathered hands cradled a gold-colored stopwatch, which, like many of the items in the store, made him appear wealthy. He wore a rose-colored badge on the pocket of his shirt.

The two men greeted each other with a smile like that of old friends. "Surprised to see you in here, Mr. Mayor," Artelius said with weary eyes.

Pierce smiled before turning away. "I'm not the mayor anymore." He walked over to the main display case in the middle of the tiny store, and scanned through the collection of rings before him. He zeroed in on one in particular with a shiny, pale gold band with several small diamonds rather than one large rock.

Artelius followed him and stood on the other side of the display case. "Thinking about marriage? It's Suzanne, right?"

Pierce lifted his gaze. "Right. I can't imagine being with anyone else. Considering all we've been through together."

"So why aren't you mayor anymore? I can't thank you enough for taking out that machine that was terrorizing us."

"Don't you watch the news?"

Artelius burst into laughter. "No. I get enough propaganda every time I use the Network Archives."

"Kalen Rusk, the CEO of Dexler has taken over." Pierce pulled the food badge button out of his pocket. "He's the one issuing these."

Artelius looked down at his own badge and then back up at Pierce. "I was going to ask you about those. What's with the colors?"

"Some kind of sorting system. I hope you don't think I'm prying, but do you go to church?"

Artelius' eyes narrowed. "Every week. Why?"

It was then that Pierce remembered hearing long, rambling tales that Artelius told him about distant relatives that lived through the Holocaust of World War II back on Earth. "I think it's based on your beliefs. I hope I'm wrong."

Artelius became pale and his hands twitched.

Pierce pointed back toward the display case. "Can I see that one?"

Artelius withdrew the ring from the case and held it out to him. Pierce turned it over and over in his hands and his heart settled on it in an instant. The other rings in the display case became unimportant and faded from view. He handed it back to Artelius with a knowing smile.

"I'll wrap this up for you," Artelius said.

Artelius withdrew a burgundy-colored, felt-lined box from behind the counter and set the ring inside. He then rang up the purchase on a video plate that sat on the counter and doubled as a cash register. "So how are you and Suzanne getting along these days?"

"Pretty well."

"Has she tested you yet?"

"Tested me?"

"Sure. By asking you if you really love her or seeing if you'd drop everything to be with her."

"She hasn't said anything like that yet. And I do love her. I can't see myself with anyone else. Besides, she's not that kind of girl."

Artelius gave him a wry look.

After Pierce exchanged credits with Artelius, he picked up the box and tucked it into his pocket. He had no specific date or time in mind for his proposal, but he knew if events in the city took a sudden turn for the worse, he would have to act quickly on his dreams.

As Pierce turned toward the door, Artelius called out to him. "Say, I have a question. Before you go."

Pierce knew that could be the start of a long and rambling conversation that Artelius was prone to begin, but tonight he decided to just ride it out. Besides, he could see a look of great concern in the man's pale eyes.

Artelius reached underneath the counter and withdrew a white, square plastic box. Across the box top in diagonal silver letters was the word, "Arena". He lifted the cover off of the box to reveal a game board and several plastic pieces. Some of the pieces were shaped like miniature gladiators with swords and others like mechanized lions. He opened up the game board to reveal a circular playing area that resembled the city Coliseum down the street.

Pierce looked up at Artelius.

"They wanted me to sell this one to the kids. I refused," the jeweler said.

"Who are they?"

"A lady came into the store with it. I thought she was just a manufacturer's rep or a designer. Turns out she was on the City Council. Can you believe that?"

"Arielle," Pierce said as he stared on at the illustrated crowds that filled the seats of the Arena game board.

"You know her?"

"Too well. I wonder what they're planning."

"I don't know. But I'm getting too old for this crap."

"Thinking about retiring?"

"I'm well on my way to that. I want to hop the next rocket back to Earth if I can help it. I miss the sounds of the ocean. Maybe I'll retire on a coast somewhere."

Artelius looked down at the badge on his denim shirt and then picked up one of the plastic lions. He twirled it about with his hand as if it reminded him of something. "You don't think this is supposed to get the kids thinking about gladiator games do you? Do you think they're going to hold them for real in the Coliseum?"

"I'm sure it's just a game." Pierce turned back toward the door to leave again. As he passed by the display window to the right of the front door, he spotted some more children's games including a chess board with holographic pieces and an odd-looking set of five cobalt-blue dice.

"Take care," Artelius said as Pierce left the store. "And watch out for the tests."

* * *

At home, Pierce squirreled the ring box away behind a hardcover atlas of the Earth in his bookshelf. He returned to the living room and activated the wall telescreen before settling onto the sofa. He caught the end of a newscast and stared on in shock as the footage showed a homemade video from inside of a warehouse. There, a stack of paper books was being burned. Like kids around a campfire, two onlookers threw more books into the fire although one could not see their faces from the camera angle. The voiceover on the telescreen said the books being burned were "religious".

Pierce knew that only meant one thing: the few paper Bibles that were brought up to the settlements were being burned. He paced up to the screen. He stared at the books, and sure enough, many of them looked to be covered in black leather or had crosses on them before being incinerated. Burning permits within the city were highly regulated and he knew from his short time as mayor who was on the list of permit holders. Yet both of the characters onscreen wore black knit masks over their faces.

The newscast then cut to a commercial, which showed an image of the giant clock that was raised up earlier in the day on the side of the City Center building. The clock hands remained pointed at the number twelve, but as the commercial carried on, the hands began to whirl rapidly around the face, hour by hour. Underneath that, the words "High Noon in Magnopolis" appeared. The commercial then cut to a scene of Kalen Rusk sitting at a work desk with a cowboy hat in his hands. Kalen had black, wavy, shoulder-length hair, an athletic upper body, and narrow eyes that hid a world of lies well.

"Hello, fellow citizens of Magnopolis," Kalen said. "I want you to get yourselves ready for a series of endeavors, entertainment, and prizes that'll be coming your way. Stay tuned because in the coming days I'll personally reveal the first of our endeavors right here on your telescreen."

Pierce felt a headache coming on. As soon as the commercial began it was over. *First the badges and now the clock*, he thought. He knew the opening of the Towers of Venice of casino was tomorrow, and so a part of him reasoned away this latest telescreen stunt as being part of that. Yet the western look Kalen sported did not fit together with anything the casino seemed to be doing.

He then switched the telescreen to the Network search screen and pulled up the official Dexler Corporation charter for the governance of Magnopolis. It was a dry, lengthy document full of amendments that could bore the most devoted political science student to sleep.

He skipped down to the section on City Council governance and found that the Council could be dissolved by the mayor if circumstances warranted it. With Arielle handing out food badges, it was unclear whether such an action would ever be taken.

Further on in the document, he studied the description of the CEO's role and its relation to the mayor. One slippery clause gave Kalen all the authority he needed: "Should emergency circumstances arise, such as martial law or the need to restore civil order, or the mayor is incapacitated, the CEO has authority to overrule or supersede the office of mayor on a temporary or permanent basis."

Although the statement stirred his anger further, it was too late now to reverse course. He thought about stirring up public unrest to support his case, but he knew Kalen would only turn that against him.

Pierce then flipped through pages and pages of news articles about himself, most of which contained erroneous details surrounding the takedown of Io and his return to the city. Much of the material was twisted and corrupt or littered with hearsay. He heard once that there is never anything random about what God does, but if this was God at work, a lot of explanation would be needed. Despite this belief, he still felt like he had to make things right. He wrestled non-stop with these thoughts until he exhausted himself and returned back to his bedroom to crash for the night.

Chapter Three

When Pierce woke up, he went straight back to the living room to check the Network Archives again. He tossed and turned all night in restless fits of sleep because his mind could not put the badge idea to rest. He pulled his food badge off of one of the side tables next to the sofa and held it in his hands. Despite not wanting to initially bring it into his house, he still wanted to test a theory of his that had percolated in his thoughts overnight.

He activated the telescreen with his voice and then directed it to search for the word "God" in the Network Archives. He braced himself for yet another drop in numbers but the number returned on the screen startled him.

The screen remained blank for a moment, and then returned the number zero.

"Bible," he called out to the screen.

The screen responded back with a few dozen results, but none of them appeared to refer to the Christian version of the Bible.

"Jesus."

Again, the screen replied with zero results.

In disbelief, he glared at his badge. It was no longer the pale yellow color it was yesterday and instead it was deep yellow with a hint of orange.

At first, he thought it was a trick of the lighting in the room. When he stepped outside, the same color difference was evident. As he stared at the badge and then at the artificial grass that filled his yard he thought twice about ever using the Network again for anything. He walked out to where his walkway met the street curb. He crouched down and stared along the length of the curb for the tiny black sensors that he noticed while standing in the food badge line with Suzanne. There were a few, but not as many as he had seen on other streets of the city.

Behind him and down the street he heard a man talking and walking. He looked back to see a man in his mid-thirties, with blue jeans and a gray sweatshirt with the hood drawn over his head. The man stared up toward a street light and then back down at the road. The entire time he talked to himself.

Pierce waited until the man approached. The man lifted off his hood and revealed his crew cut, sandy-brown hair. Pierce immediately recognized him as his friend Kyrk. "Everything okay?"

Kyrk smiled and nodded up toward another nearby street light. He mouthed the words "we're being recorded" without a sound.

Pierce nodded but did not fully understand.

Kyrk spoke up. "Say, have you heard about Camp Io?"

"What's that?"

Kyrk shook his head from side to side with urgency and put a finger to his lips. "I hear Camp Io is where the rebels are gathering. They say the base is far out of range of the Sentinels and the city cameras."

Pierce nodded his head slower this time and stepped back from Kyrk a few feet. He planned on going over to Suzanne's house anyway and now looked to be as good a time as any to get moving.

Kyrk caught him by shirt sleeve and leaned over to whisper in his ear. "By the way, there is no Camp Io. But we do have a plan. Well, Omar and I have a plan."

Pierce grinned and noticed Kyrk's badge was a pale yellow orange color. He wondered how long that would last if all their words were being recorded as Kyrk claimed. In the distance, he heard the telltale whirring sound of an approaching Sentinel and at that point, he departed for Suzanne's house.

* * *

As he neared the Towers of Venice Casino, he noticed it was opening day for the establishment, and by the looks of it, half of the city was crammed inside. Gondola rides with passengers circulated along canals that encompassed the building. The gondoliers were dressed in burgundy-colored pants with puffy white dress shirts and drove the gondolas along with slender aluminum poles. A line of people stood just outside the front door of the building as if it was

Michael Galloway

somehow a portal back to the planet Earth.

As Pierce walked past, he heard shouts inside and soon a fight broke out. Two men in their early twenties were escorted out by a bouncer that was twice each man's size, but they carried on their argument outside. The bouncer pursued them off of the property and away from Pierce. He wondered how long it would be before this became a nightly event.

Once he arrived at Suzanne's door, he pressed the doorbell and waited. He removed his badge from his shirt and dropped it into the waterless grass, and just to the right of her door. Her yard was empty now, but months ago it had been populated with strange ornamental statues and gadgets built by her eclectic late husband Timothy. One sculpture was a busy tangle of wire, springs, and triangular pieces of copper while another was a human statue carved out of basalt that looked toward the sky. Suzanne told him the artifacts were now in storage since they were too painful to look at anymore.

She opened the door and gave him a warm smile. "I see you're living recklessly." She pointed toward his chest where his food badge was supposed to be.

He returned a smile and ducked inside. "It doesn't look like you have a badge on either. Let's get together sometime."

Suzanne's house was filled with the aroma of spaghetti and meatballs, which put Pierce at ease again. He looked around the living room to find James on the floor with a handheld computing device in one hand and a food badge in the other. James set the badge onto the plush gray carpet and then pointed the device at it.

"What's today's project?" He asked James as he knelt down next to the boy.

James looked up and smiled. "It's a scrambling device. I'm trying to see if I can change a badge color with a remote control."

Pierce's mind reeled with the possibilities and uses for that. If his own badge changed subtly just by accessing the Network, much like Kyrk's badge did, then there had to be some type of wireless contact going on between the Network and the badges. He was sure such communications were encrypted, but the thinness of the badge left little physical room for shielding from outside interference. Given enough time, he knew James would probably figure something out even if it involved brute algorithmic force.

He stood up and followed Suzanne into the kitchen and gave her a kiss on the cheek. "Have you looked at the Network lately?"

"Just for the news. Why?"

"Something big is up. Remember what I told you in the past about words and phrases being slowly taken out of the Archives? They're gone now."

Suzanne stirred the spaghetti sauce in a metal pan on the stovetop but stopped as soon as Pierce finished talking. She set the spoon onto a ceramic plate on the counter and turned to face him. She glanced over his shoulder at James in the living room and lowered her voice to a whisper.

"Everything's gone?"

Pierce nodded. "And my badge color changed when I went searching for the missing words. It's not plain yellow anymore."

The color drained out of her face as she stared at her own badge which sat on top of the kitchen table.

Pierce did not see any change in her badge since the night before. He did not see a point in testing his searching theory on her badge. He could see by the look in her eyes that she understood what was happening and maybe had a better handle on the ramifications than he did.

He reached over to turn off one of the other stove burners where the spaghetti noodles boiled in a pot. "Don't worry. They can take God out of the Network Archives but they can't take Him out of the equation. They can try all they want to take away the meaning of life but it'll never work."

Suzanne pulled out a colander from the cupboard and set it into the sink. She then poured the pot full of noodles into it. "They can't do this to us."

"They won't win at this, Sue. You know that, right? Tomorrow I think I'm going to stop in at the new casino. To try and get a reading from people on the street."

"Be careful. You're not the mayor anymore."

"I'm not worried. It's not like everyone has turned on us yet."

Chapter Four

After the opening day crowds departed, Pierce stepped into the Towers of Venice casino. The lines that clogged the entryway yesterday were gone, but it still looked like half the city tried to fit inside. Once he entered the lobby, he was struck by the opulence of the facility. The main hallway was lined with gold-colored pillars with an arched ceiling that was covered in paintings and illustrations reminiscent of the Renaissance Era back on Earth. Illustrations of Da Vinci machines were complimented by Michelangelo-type paintings. In the middle of the hallway was a female sculpture covered in gold that held up a wire globe that resembled Mars.

Side hallways led to various areas such as a bar, blackjack tables, and slot machines. Casinos always made him edgy, and today was no exception. As he passed through, he could overhear the monotonous electronic drone of the slot machines as they hypnotized the patrons with alluring precision.

He stepped inside of an elevator and rode up to the second floor. There, he passed by a small concert hall where he caught a glimpse of a fully mechanized band made up of programmed robots. Their music was a complex mathematical symphony of guitars and drums, punctuated by fleeting synthesizer chords. He walked over to the lounge and in a moment of concern, he checked his badge color, but could not tell if any changes occurred due to the dim lighting inside.

The lounge was a dark contrast to the gold-colored excess of the first floor. The walls, carpeting, tables, and chairs here were black or burgundy. Even the wait staff wore black pants except for their white shirts which made them stand out. The atmosphere felt crowded, dark, and made Pierce wonder how many shady deals happening in the shadows.

In the back of the lounge, he found Reed Zimmer from the Recon Department sitting alone at a table and off to the side. Reed was in his mid-fifties, with a dark bronze complexion, a fading head of gray and black hair, and a sharp mustache. He walked with a cane but his strength came in the form of numerical ability, wisdom, and detective skills. As Pierce approached, he gave Reed a wave, all the while staring at Reed's badge, which looked to be a pale yellow color or even plain white.

"What brings you here?" Reed asked as he leaned forward and extended a hand to shake.

"I need your advice. Being an ex-mayor and all that, I hope Kalen hasn't ordered you not to speak to me."

Reed turned to the side and chuckled. "Oh, he hasn't. Or if he did, I didn't see the memo." Reed motioned toward the empty chair on the other side of the table. "Take a seat."

Pierce sat down and grabbed a hold of his food badge which was attached to his shirt. "Whose idea was this? These aren't just for food, are they?"

Reed hesitated a moment and then downed the remainder of his dark beer. He motioned toward a waitress. "They don't resemble the identity badges we had in storage do they?"

"Some have red badges, some have orange. Then I noticed the color changed when I accessed specific things on the Network. Is everything being recorded now? Even this conversation?"

Reed shifted in his chair and looked Pierce in the eye. "Look. I don't know what Kalen has planned, but I know the badges are part of some kind of monitoring system. And sometime tonight there will be more monitors out on the streets. Those were his orders. If you ask me, I think it is overkill."

"What kind of monitors? Cyclodes?"

"No. Busybees. And they aren't out to gather pollen or make honey."

Pierce leaned forward. "You lost me."

Reed lifted up his right hand and held his thumb and forefinger an inch apart. "A busybee is a flying device about this big. Some are just dumb monitors that try to pick up on radio communications while others have a camera and a microphone."

Pierce took a deep breath and looked back across the lounge toward the elevator. "They're not going to follow me into my house, right?" He let out a nervous chuckle. "I suppose it's no worse than the bugs in the streetlights or the receptors embedded in the street curbs."

"You're pretty observant. So what are you doing to keep busy these days?"

"Waiting for the other shoe to drop." Pierce looked around the casino lounge and listened to the clink of glasses behind the bar and the distant beats of the robot band. For some reason, Reed was no longer being his usual talkative self tonight. He wondered if their conversation was being monitored from above or from a nearby table.

He cleared his throat. "Have you heard anything about an ongoing rebellion?"

Reed flashed a thin smile but then became quite serious. "I wouldn't worry about that."

"Right. Because once we took down Io that ended, correct?"

Reed lifted an eyebrow.

Pierce charged ahead. "I find it amazing after all I did that this is how things ended up."

"Sometimes people have to do what's best for the city. To some what you did was considered reckless abandonment in a crisis. If anything, you should have stayed back, but instead you were a hothead that wasted company resources."

"I rescued Suzanne and another employee."

"While risking everyone else's safety?"

"And I do it all over again." Pierce stood up to leave.

"What's the hurry?" Reed said, startled. The waitress arrived with another dark beer for him, which looked like a Guinness beer imported from Earth.

"Tomorrow is Sunday, right? I think I need a good way to spend my down time. Maybe meet up with some real rebels. I'll see you around."

"Be careful of rebellion talk, Pierce. If you ask me…"

"I did ask you," he replied with a tinge of sarcasm in his voice. "I asked you about a lot of things. For someone who practically built the Recon Department from the ground up, you suddenly don't seem to know anything."

Before Reed could reply, Pierce waved goodbye and then left via the elevator. On his way back out onto the street, he scanned the domed sky for signs of electronic monitoring insects. Although he did not see anything flying around in the casino, he knew there were cameras everywhere and that the information was likely being filtered back toward the Network servers through whatever algorithms Kalen had in place. Who knew how the data was being twisted and warped or what the system would assemble about his character from the past few days. There was cold comfort as he looked down at his badge and noticed it had not changed color over the past hour.

As he approached his home, he pulled a video plate out of his pocket and called Suzanne. "Good evening, my love."

"How are you?" She said in a warm, thoughtful voice. Her eyes grabbed a hold of his as he held the plate out in front of him. He paced up the walkway toward his front door.

It was then that he heard a faint noise in the distance, behind him, and high up in the air. He wheeled around to look and saw a black cloud of dots above an adjacent neighborhood. The dots moved as one, like a swarm of real bees, and then dispersed as if it was nothing more than a wisp of smoke.

He turned back to face the video plate but could hear the sound of quiet buzzing behind him. To his right he watched an electronic bee swoop and dart over the neighbor's house and then disappear.

"Everything okay?" She said, worried at his silence.

He ducked inside of his home and shut the front door. He leaned against a living room wall, tore off his badge, and threw it across the room. It ricocheted off the telescreen wall and skittered back across the floor and under the sofa. "Yeah. I met with Reed tonight. From Recon." He shook his head.

"What is it?"

"I think Kalen got to him. He wouldn't tell me anything. Oh, and I found out we've got some new visitors now. They look like bees but record like cameras. Busybees, he called them. I'll bet they planned this months ago…"

Suzanne bit her lip. "Where are you?"

"I'm at home. But I'd stay indoors until I figure these things out. I'll let you know what I find out. You up for church in the morning?"

"I haven't been to one in a very long time. You mean the one in the middle of town, right?"

Pierce nodded. "It's a nice place. The pastor is a real nice guy, too."

"Okay, we'll join you. I don't know about Lisabeth, but at least

James and I will go. We could all use a break, I think."

After Pierce ended the call he looked out his front window. He did not see any more flying bugs around, but he knew they were probably not far off. His heart raced with the possibilities and his mind struggled with the absurdity of it all. He called out to the wall telescreen.

"Busybees," he said aloud.

The results that filled his screen in the next few seconds made him long to take the first flight back to Earth. What surprised him even more was that so much information was publicly available. One of the first articles he examined contained multiple images and diagrams of the device, which was modeled to look like a real bumblebee from Earth. Each bee had a set of wings, was equipped with black-and-white cameras, and had a flight time of two hours at most. They could hover above crowds of people and could gather or disperse like a real swarm. Despite the flowery descriptions and biased articles he could not discern a good logical reason for their deployment.

It was then he remembered Kalen's talk as he rescued Suzanne from the clutches of the mountainous Chronopticus prison. Kalen talked of having created an all-seeing time machine which analyzed, sifted, and sorted through information on every citizen in the settlements in a desperate search to find patterns and maybe even predict the future. Kalen also referenced something called the Eden Project and Pierce doubted it had the same definition as the Biblical version.

Was everyone in the settlements trapped inside a giant machine? How long would it be before a method was developed to read their every thought? Were they all being brooded over like rats in a psychology experiment?

He glanced up again at the telescreen which sat before him cold, motionless, and muted. "Eden Project," he said aloud to the screen, and waited.

Chapter Five

Pierce walked with Suzanne and James up the front stairs of the city church near the center of downtown Magnopolis. As other churchgoers approached and entered the building, he studied their badge colors with great interest. He was not surprised to see most of the badges were either crimson or various shades of orange. He looked on again at his own badge and suddenly felt out of place.

The building was one of the few he admired in the city for its architecture. The exterior was off-white, with an emphasis on vertical lines that were accented by silver coloring. The foundation was made of Martian sandstone, and although there were only two stories to the building, the streamlined look of it made it appear taller than it really was.

Pierce looked around them and kept an eye out for the busybees Reed spoke of in the casino. He leaned over and whispered in Suzanne's ear. "I wonder how they monitor this place? Do you think our badge colors will change as the service goes on?"

"I hope not. Although ours look really out of place, don't they? James' is the brightest of them all. It's practically pure white."

They shuffled inside to find an impressive interior that reflected the design aesthetic of the exterior. The spacious sanctuary held only two hundred seats from what Pierce remembered, but many of the pews were full. He did not know how the numbers compared to a typical Sunday.

They slipped into the back of the sanctuary and took their seats in silence. There were no books in the pews which struck Pierce as odd. Back on Earth it was not uncommon to see Bibles, songbooks, or other material lining the rack on the back of each pew. Many congregations switched over to portable reading devices or holographic popup screens attached to the back of each pew. In the front of the sanctuary stood a black marble altar covered in a white linen cloth. On top of the altar were two golden candle holders with lit white candles on either side of a large opened Bible. Off to the left, a six-member choir dressed in black and white robes kicked off the service with a hymn. For a time, Pierce felt as if they were all an island of peace in a sea of bureaucratic, ideological, and societal uncertainty.

After the readings from the Bible were completed, Pastor Capshaw stepped out from behind his podium and walked out to the landing that stood just in front of the stone altar. As the pastor launched into his sermon, Pierce felt a nudge on his side.

He turned to see what Suzanne was looking at. There, in the back of the sanctuary, near the exit, stood Kalen Rusk. Dressed in a black suit with a crimson tie, he leaned casually against the back wall as if he waited for the proper timing. Kalen's eyes focused straight ahead on the pastor, and Pierce looked to see the pastor nervously looking back toward Kalen. Pierce did not know how long Kalen stood there, but he was sure Kalen did not arrive with the initial crowd at the beginning of the service. The smile on Kalen's face was creepy at best and his eyes darted from Pastor Capshaw to a gold pocket watch in his hand. Pierce had not seen a pocket watch with a chain like that in a decade and a pale blue glow emanating from its face.

At once, Kalen flipped the cover of the pocket watch closed and slipped it into the upper breast pocket of his suit coat. Pierce turned back to watch Pastor Capshaw.

"...and so in our readings for today we come to passage where David is hiding from King Saul," the pastor continued.

At that point Kalen strutted down the center aisle between the two main rows of pews and up to the front of the sanctuary. There was an unspoken arrogance and swagger to his demeanor. Pastor Capshaw cleared his throat twice.

"Excuse me, can I help you?" Pastor Capshaw said, his voice shaking.

Kalen did not answer until he reached the front and stood next to the pastor as if they were giving the sermon together. He kept his hands in his pants pockets and then stared out across the audience who sat in rapt shock and silence. "That's a cute story you're telling. But does anyone really believe it here?"

"I should certainly hope they would..."

"Because it came from your mouth? Because you threaten and intimidate these people with your make-believe ideas of hell?" Kalen continued to survey the crowd until he locked on to Pierce's eyes.

Pierce turned to Suzanne. "Okay. He's gone too far now."

Kalen glared at Pastor Capshaw. "What if I came in here today and told you that I was a god? What if I could show your congregation their past, present, and future all at once?" He reached into his pocket and withdrew a metal orb the size of a golf ball and pitched it straight up into the air. The orb burst apart into a cloud of a thousand tiny blue and silver mirrors. The mirrors rained down to the floor and left behind an illuminated image of the pastor.

"How much does your congregation *really* love you, Pastor? Do they know your real past? Do they know the *real* you? Would they still stand up for you if they knew what you were like before you arrived here in Magnopolis?"

Pastor Capshaw shifted his feet and backed away from Kalen and the holographic image of himself. The image shifted from a current one of the pastor to a three-dimensional snapshot of the man as a teenager.

Kalen held a small, black control device in one hand and aimed it at the image. It changed to show the teenager as he reached into the backseat of a vehicle and withdrew a paper bag with a bottle inside. The teenager took a drink off the bottle before setting it back into the backseat. "Where do we start? Let's see. This one was picked up by a camera inside of your parents' car," he said in a snarky tone of voice. "I think this one speaks for itself. But let's fast forward a bit."

Kalen clicked his controller again.

"Please stop this," Pastor Capshaw said.

"Why? Isn't this about the truth? Or what is truth for you?"

"I'm not like that anymore," he said, adjusting the rope on his robe. "My mind and my life have been transformed."

"Have they? A few years after this, we have this little nugget."

The image before them changed from that of a teenager to one of the pastor as a young man, probably in his twenties, walking along a beach. He approached a camera attached to a food vendor booth next to the beach. The view showed him reaching up and covering the camera, but the cloth he used was blown off by the wind. It then switched to a view of him sneaking inside the closed-up shack and fixing himself a sandwich. Finally, it showed him picking open the lock on the cash register till and pulling out a few bills.

Pastor Capshaw blushed and cleared his throat. "I never did that again either. I was broke at the time and hadn't eaten in a day. I got desperate."

"So what you're saying is, in a moment of desperation you broke your own rules."

"I wasn't a Christian yet."

"Convenient. Let's take a look at what you've done as a pastor up here."

"Stop," shouted a voice from the set of pews to the right of Pierce. Ruelle Dorner stood up and stared at Kalen. "What do you think you're doing?"

Pierce rose to his feet. Suzanne looked up toward him and tugged at his shirt sleeve but he refused to sit down.

Although Kalen glared at Ruelle, he also kept an eye on Pierce. An eerie smile broke across his face as he held out his hand toward the holographic image. The image collapsed in on itself and streamed back up into his hand until it condensed back into a silver orb. He pocketed the orb and put his hands behind his back. "I came here today to demonstrate something to you. I came here to show the kind of power I can wield now. It's a power that anyone can wield." He faced Pastor Capshaw for a moment. "Even you, Pastor."

"You don't get it, do you?" Ruelle said with boldness in her voice. She gripped the railing on the pew in front of her tight enough to make it creak.

"Oh, I get it. For centuries people have preached out of your musty book. And what has it brought? Peace? I don't see that. I see war. I see division. I see confinement. I'm here today to tell you that I've become a god overnight. Oh, and I can travel through time and see from beginning to end all at the press of a button. Can you do that?"

"You can leave now," Pierce said, just loud enough for Kalen to hear him. After the words left his lips, he wondered if he said the right thing. He could feel a chill wash over himself as the hair stood on the back of his neck.

Kalen brushed off the comment with a chuckle. "Okay." He faced the pastor one last time before he turned toward the back of the sanctuary. "But tomorrow, we'll all find out how much your congregation really loves you, Pastor. Tomorrow, we'll see where their loyalty really lies."

He playfully tapped the pastor on the shoulder with his fist, but the pastor recoiled in horror. "My money is on themselves."

In an attempt to compose himself, Pastor Capshaw recited a verse from memory. "A fool says in his heart there is no God." The pastor shook and his eyes burned with a mixture of fear and indignation.

Kalen continued toward the exit and shook his head. He left the sanctuary without another word. Ruelle continued to stand and moved out of the pew and walked toward the front in a show of support for the pastor.

Pierce sat down and watched as several others stepped forward to stand in a tight circle around the pastor. Soon, Ruelle led them in a prayer for Kalen, themselves, and the church.

After the service, many people in the congregation shook hands with the pastor, while Pierce, Suzanne, and James slipped out the side exit. Suzanne and Pierce held hands with one another and headed back toward her house at the edge of the city.

Behind them, Pierce heard the mechanical sound of a Cyclode Sentinel in motion, although it was quieter than usual. He spun around and watched as a Sentinel moved toward the church they had just left. Although the machine was the same height as a typical Cyclode Sentinel, its design was more fluid and the coloring was white and pale blue instead of silver and blue.

"What is it?" Suzanne said as she turned around to look.

"New Sentinels. They call them S3s. I wonder when those arrived."

As he studied the design from a distance, a buzzing sound passed above them and continued on toward the church. He looked up to see a dozen busybees flying in a v-formation straight toward the steeple. When they reached the steeple, they formed a circle and hovered above it like a blackened halo.

"Looks like we have visitors," Pierce said. He checked his badge and noticed it was now a pale orange color.

Chapter Six

The following morning, Pierce awoke to the sound of the door buzzer. He rubbed his eyes and walked into the living room. When he opened the door, he was surprised to find Suzanne standing there.

"I thought you were supposed to be at work. Is everything okay?" He said as he stood in the doorway. "Here, come in."

"I can't, or I'll be late. I just wanted to let you know that Lisabeth told me about something happening today. She heard from one of her co-workers that several new Sentinels have moved into the city and taken up patrol positions and checkpoints again." She reached out and grabbed his hand, but Pierce decided to turn it into a kiss and a hug instead.

"Do you want me to escort you to work?" He said.

"No, I'll be okay. But call me if anything breaks. Or I'll call you."

Pierce nodded and for a moment did not want to let her go. His mind began to race with thoughts of her safety. When he did let her go, it felt like the day she left for the mission to track down the five missing crates that landed on the planet when the first settlers arrived.

As she headed back to the street, he admired her a moment and then slid the front door shut. Although she was employed by a company name Donner Systems, that company was contracted by the Dexler Corporation. She worked as a hardware and network installation technician for small businesses, but they both knew if she suddenly lost her job, they had savings to fall back on.

He turned his attention back toward the living room telescreen, as there were items that he wanted to research before setting out on a trip to the local store to pick up supplies. Although he knew that his purchases would be tracked, a part of him did not care anymore. Besides, if Kalen wanted to stand in the middle of a church and declare himself to be God, that meant he would immediately alienate a portion of the city and others throughout the settlements. This time, he felt, Kalen had gone too far in threatening a popular citizen in Pastor Capshaw. The church had withstood other antics over the years ever since its construction and Pierce felt this challenge was no different.

He withdrew his city plan notebook from a nearby end table drawer and flipped through a few pages of its contents. It helped to spark his imagination and keep his dreams alive, if only for a few minutes a day. He then withdrew the other paper notebook which tracked search results from the Network Archives. The zero results the other day for words related to God startled him, but he knew there had to be more to the story than a few empty searches. He brought up the telescreen to search, but before he could use it, it was interrupted by an emergency message.

He tried changing channels, but every one of them played the same message. It was yet another announcement from Kalen. If he somehow topped the stunt he pulled yesterday, Pierce thought, it would be remarkable.

An image of Kalen filled the screen. It showed him standing downtown and in front of the City Center building. "When the pioneers first settled this planet, they had a set of goals in mind. Their first goal was to survive and to that end, they succeeded admirably. Their second goal was progress for civilization as a whole. Yet today the work on that second goal remains unfinished. That goal has been passed to future generations to tend to."

Pierce grimaced and then took a seat on the sofa. He took furious notes in his search results notebook.

Kalen continued. "Unfortunately, some of the original settlers brought ideas that should have been left back on Earth. Like a town in the Old West, those ideas led to trouble. And like those old towns, with trouble comes a need for law and order. A way to round up outlaws if you know what I mean."

Kalen gestured toward the sky. The camera panned up to reveal the giant analog clock that had been erected on the side of the City Center building a few days ago. The face of the clock was now lit up and its edge radiated a bluish-white neon glow. The hands emitted a similar bluish-white glow, but still pointed straight up toward the number twelve.

The camera zoomed out to show both Kalen and the clock as he held his right hand toward the clock face. The piercing gaze in his eyes intensified. "As a result, and on behalf of the leadership of Magnopolis, I would like to introduce a new endeavor. We're calling this High Noon."

As soon as Pierce heard the words, he stopped writing in his notebook. He crossed his arms and waited for the next punch. Behind and to the right of Kalen hung a black, white, and red poster for an organization called the Dove League. The poster showed two hands extending out in a welcoming gesture.

"The hands on this clock will remain pointed at noon for the duration of this endeavor. But around the city we have installed whistles that will sound at the beginning and the end of the endeavor. Now here are the rules. And the rules are simple." The camera closed in on Kalen's face. "Identify those with red badges and turn them into the authorities. The reward? Fifty food credits per turn in and a special 100 credits for Pastor Capshaw. Why red badges? These folks have been identified by the Network as standing in the way of progress. It's our duty to reeducate them."

Kalen then glanced down at his suit pocket and withdrew the pocket watch he carried yesterday into the city church. He flipped open the lid and then held up his left hand to his ear. "Are you ready?" The sound of a steam whistle blowing came through the telescreen. Pierce could also hear the sound faintly through his living room walls.

"That's the sound I like to hear. And remember, may the algorithms watch over you."

At that the broadcast ended. Pierce's breathing intensified as he picked up his video plate and dialed Suzanne. Before he could introduce himself, she answered.

"I heard," she said.

"Did you make it to work okay?"

"Barely. But everybody here is nervous. I don't think anyone here has a badge color like that."

Pierce only nodded his head and then glanced around the room. "I think it's time to prepare."

"To leave?"

He nodded her off.

"To fight?"

He gave her a mischievous grin, but she did not reply. She only bit her lower lip.

"Don't you agree?" He said.

"Maybe we should leave."

"Where would we go?"

"I don't know. Maybe the Freeland settlement. Or La Crescent to the..." She stopped in mid-sentence. Her face became pale as she looked over her shoulder to see if anyone was listening.

"We'll talk later. I'll see you when you get done with work." He gave her a reassuring smile but inside he felt like everything was coming apart again.

As he hung up on the call, he peered out through his living room window. The streets, like usual, were quiet. He did not see any busybees in flight or any of the new Sentinel machines prowling the neighborhood. Yet he knew the character of the neighborhood and of the city was about to take a turn for the worse.

He flipped through a few channels on the telescreen and stopped on one news channel in particular. Across the bottom of the screen the scrolling text headlines mentioned that the city church in the middle of downtown was now officially closed. He knew it was not Pastor Capshaw's idea, as he would have held a rally there if nothing else. The images onscreen changed to that of the front doors of the church, which were now sealed with a metallic disc imprinted with the letters "DC" on it. In the background, two new Sentinel S3 machines stood watch. Plastered on the wall of the church next to the front doors was another Dove League poster. This one showed the same two hands extended outward with a slogan along the bottom that read: "Peace Through Reeducation."

Pierce turned off the telescreen and paced into his bedroom. From his desk drawer he withdrew the lone ion coil pistol he owned. It fit comfortably in the palm of his hand and the metallic coiled end piece rested along his fingertips. He knew that with the complete loss of control of the Cyclodes that it put any resistance efforts at a great disadvantage. One well placed pistol shot could do substantial damage, but against ion-coil-hardened machines it was mostly worthless.

He thought about doing weapons design searches on the Network, but he was sure that act alone would change the color of his badge.

His mind raced with ideas for building homemade weapons, but he knew so little about ballistics and electronics that it would likely be an exercise in frustration.

He returned to the living room and pulled up the Network search screen again. The first image he brought up was a street map of Magnopolis. He then sat down on the sofa and withdrew a notebook from the drawer on the end table. He flipped to a blank page and began copying down the map from the screen.

Next, he pulled up maps of Westfield, Freeland, and the La Crescent settlements and copied those into the notebook. At the end, he turned off the telescreen and marked off the houses on the Magnopolis map of where each City Council member lived. Then he marked off places to avoid. He sketched out possible areas to trap the Cyclodes should the situation devolve into street battles.

Although he had a pile of rocket scrap metal in storage and he had enough carpentry skills to build himself a bookcase, he was at a loss on how to bring a single machine down. *Perhaps Suzanne really did have a point*, he thought to himself. Soon, he found himself looking hard at the exits of the city, the distances to each one from their houses, and how far it was to each of the other settlements. *Maybe Artelius had it right all along. Not only was it time to leave, but maybe it was time to go back to Earth.*

Chapter Seven

Pierce headed out to Suzanne's house but all the way there he kept checking over his shoulder. He did not see many busybees flying about and his walk between their homes was calm and uneventful. It was too quiet, he reasoned, since the opening whistle of High Noon earlier in the day. The Sentinel patrols seemed routine, although he half thought about walking by the Pastor's home to see what was happening there. He struggled to maintain focus and more than once the thought came to him that the authorities were going to start transporting people to the prison complex where Suzanne was once held.

By the time he arrived, Suzanne opened the door and greeted him with a hug and a kiss. It was a relief to see her, he thought, and to hold her in his arms again. He could tell by the look in her eyes, though, that she was hard at work on the solution to their problem.

As he entered her living room, he found James sitting cross-legged on the floor, tinkering with some wires on his badge scrambler. Next to him were a handful of cobalt-blue dice like the ones Pierce saw in Artelius' store. A few feet away from that was James' food badge, which was no longer pure white, but rather a faint yellow color. Pierce wondered if Kalen's next "endeavor" would involve going after the lighter-colored badges.

Pierce sat down on the sofa across from James and watched the boy fiddle with the electronic device. The badge changed color in an instant to bright orange and then gradually darkened to a shade of brick red before it turned violet. Then it switched to pure white. The changes brought a smile to James' face and at the flip of a switch the badge color reverted back to a pale yellow.

"I got it to work while you were on the way over," James said with a broad grin.

Pierce extended a hand and James slapped it in approval. "That's pretty incredible. I can't imagine what you could do with the right equipment." Pierce desperately wanted to take the boy under his wing like his own son, but those types of conversations were still few and far between for him and Suzanne. At times, he could sense her leading him into the role, or at least opening the door for it at some point. Early on in their relationship she wisely drew certain boundaries and although he respected those due to the loss of her husband Timothy, another part of him was ready to embrace the opportunity on a moment's notice.

Suzanne sat down next to Pierce and nudged him with an elbow. "Think this will buy us some time?"

"I hope so," Pierce said, still trying to read her eyes. "You're thinking about something, aren't you?"

Suzanne nodded. "Remember how we talked today about our conversations being tracked? I thought of something that can't be tracked by the Network. It's a flaw Kalen didn't account for."

"Our thoughts?"

"More than that. He can't track gifts. Like when he barged in on the church service. Ruelle stood up and so did you. I saw another person start to pray while Kalen was talking. His system can't account for spiritual things. It's doomed to fail."

She reached over and picked up the opened Bible that sat on the glass-topped living room table. She flipped it to the section on spiritual gifts and pointed out the passages to Pierce. He then noticed a stack of Bible-related books that she borrowed from his personal collection.

He did not have an immediate response for her since his own reading of the Bible waxed and waned with his mood. He knew of some attempts at mind reading technology over the years, but much of it relied on direct implants into the brain or devices placed around the person's skull at close range.

"I hope you're right," he continued. "In the meantime, I brought some maps. Here," he said as he pulled out his notebook. He opened it up to the street map of Magnopolis.

Just then he heard shouting coming from somewhere outside. At first he ignored it, but the shouts grew louder. Eventually, he peered out through the living room window curtains to see a man in a red shirt, a few doors down, arguing with a neighbor. Pierce would have ignored them except the argument revolved around badges. As soon as he heard the words, "High Noon", he knew he had heard enough.

"Here we go." Pierce stood up and went to the front door. It slid open at his command and he stood just inside the doorway to watch. The man with the red shirt ducked back inside of the house. The move was followed by the sounds of breaking glass as the bay window on his house collapsed into a shower of shards.

Down the block, he could see four third-generation Cyclode Sentinels marching toward the house where the argument occurred. The other neighbor, who probably called the authorities, scrambled back into his own house to hide. Overhead, a handful of busybees circle about in a frenzy.

Pierce felt Suzanne tug at his shirt sleeve as she motioned for him to come back indoors. He shrugged her off and instead watched as the machines marched up the driveway and stopped a few feet from the front door. An order was made for the man to come outside of his home but he did not comply. The order was repeated. Again, no reply came.

James snuck up alongside of Pierce and peeked out through the doorway. Suzanne called out to the both of them to come back inside, but eventually she joined them. As they watched, the lead machine fired an ion coil weapon at the front door and opened it. Shouts came from inside the house as the machine entered without abandon. Pierce clenched his fists and thought twice about running back home to retrieve his ion coil pistol.

No further shots were fired. In minutes, the man exited the house with his hands in the air and the Cyclode Sentinel behind him. Pierce caught a glimpse of the man's badge, which hung off of his jeans pocket. It was bright red in color like the man's shirt. The man turned back to exchange words with the machine behind him, but otherwise complied. He was escorted into a transport vehicle that had a considerable amount of dust on its tires, and Pierce knew in an instant where the man was going to end up.

"How did they know where the man was?" Suzanne said.

"Predictive algorithms. Remember what Kalen said about seeing through time?"

Pierce felt a heaviness fill his chest and slid the front door shut. He gave Suzanne an icy glance. "Is this what we're going to live with

35

now? House to house searches? Neighbors calling on neighbors?"

Suzanne gave Pierce a nasty glare. "James, can you go to your room a minute?"

"But I want to see what happens," James said.

"Go."

James slouched and slogged his way toward his bedroom.

"And shut the door," Suzanne yelled.

James' bedroom door slid shut.

"I wanted to show you the maps I copied," Pierce said.

"Are they escape routes? God, I can't believe I'm saying that."

"We don't have to run, Sue." He retrieved his notebook and showed her a map of Magnopolis. "On the way over here, I started to rethink things."

"What are those tick marks for?"

"Alleys where we can trap the Cyclodes."

"Then what?"

"We'll have to come up with ways to take them out."

She pointed to another set of black marks on the perimeter of the dome. "What are those?"

"Those are escape routes, but only if we need them."

"I thought your plan was to fight."

"It is. I've marked off the houses where the City Council members live."

She looked up at him with stern eyes.

"So we can avoid them. Now if we can figure out where some of the people with orange badges live, maybe we can meet somewhere and strategize."

Just then he felt a slight rumble underneath his feet. "Did you feel that?"

"It's a rocket leaving."

They both darted back to the living room window and stared out to see a diffuse pillar of rocket cloud ascending in the distance from Beta Base. As evening fell on the domed city, the panels on the roof shifted from translucency to transparency. The white cloud arced into the heavens lit atop by the orange breath of a Dragonfire rocket.

"I wonder if Artelius is heading home," Pierce said with a melancholic tone to his voice.

Chapter Eight

Two days later, Pierce escorted Suzanne home from her job near downtown. As he held her hand, he looked around and wondered how many citizens had been picked up. Would shops close and whole industries be thrown into chaos?

High above, Pierce heard a busybee following their every turn. More busybees were out tonight, almost as if one was now assigned to every person or group of people out on the street. Their increased presence irritated him since they flew several feet out of his reach but just close enough to record conversations or track movements via a video stream. "Suzanne, I should start reading more of my Bible now that I have this new free time. In addition to looking for jobs, of course." He winked at Suzanne.

She smiled back. "Wouldn't be a bad idea. My problem is that every time I start, I stop a day later because it convicts me."

"But what I really want to know about the Bible is how it all fits together. I mean, the Bible is the Word of God, right? Do you think Kalen has ever read the Bible? Do you think if he got into a Bible challenge match with Pastor Capshaw that he would stand a chance? I think we should get a hold of some more paper Bibles..."

"Are you okay tonight?" She asked in a low voice. Her mouth was partially open as she gave him a puzzled look.

He winked again at her and motioned toward the sky without looking up. He knew his emphasis on the word Bible was a little over-the-top, but it was a test to see if they really were being recorded. He looked down at his food badge, which hung from his pants pocket and tried to gauge its color.

He stopped on a street corner and lifted up his badge for a closer look. There, upon closer inspection, he found that the badge color had indeed taken on a deeper shade of orange, and he knew this was no trick of the domed sunlight radiating down from above. He half thought about repeating some Biblical concepts and phrases multiple times to see how fast he could change his badge color. Could he find himself hauled away by the end of the night if he said enough keywords?

Across the street, some new nanoparticle graffiti was written on the side of a warehouse. The graffiti was painted in a prominent cherry-red script. It read, "Help God" and soon disappeared only to reappear on another wall of the building. The phrase made little sense to him, and there appeared to be more writing on the building next to that, near Artelius' jewelry shop. The jewelry shop had a circular metal seal on its front door, just like the one he saw on the city church's doors.

Further up the block he saw a group of five boys sitting in a circle on the sidewalk playing a game of Arena. One of the boys threw a handful of cobalt-blue dice onto the street which resulted in shouts for two of the boys and complaints from the others. Pierce could see thin, white, plastic credit cards being exchanged, but one of the boys who gave up the cards looked angry and argumentative.

A fight ensued and Pierce directed the three of them to remain on their side of the street while they continued on toward the Good Mars Restaurant. Next thing they knew, dice, the game board, and plastic lions were being kicked everywhere. The street fight was not unprecedented, and they were increasing as the city remained on edge since the destruction of the ag domes.

When they entered the restaurant, they were quickly seated by a waitress. She stood five foot two and spoke with a heavy Indian accent. She directed them to sit in a booth in the front corner of the restaurant. Meanwhile, the busybee that followed them all the way from Suzanne's workplace stopped in front of the restaurant, hovered for a moment, and then buzzed away.

High up on a nearby wall, a small telescreen hung in the corner and was turned to a Network news station. Pierce stopped watching the station altogether since its coverage became more biased toward Kalen and the Dexler Corporation by the hour. He expected a news story on the new graffiti in town or some mundane mining story. Instead, several citizens who were rounded up as part of the recent "High Noon" endeavor were paraded onscreen. In the crowd he recognized the organist and an usher from the city church, along with

Artelius Gray. All of them were lined up against a wall until a Cyclode directed them into a nearby transport crawler.

"Guess Artelius didn't make it," Pierce said as the footage showed several crawlers driving away. He could not hear the audio but it did not matter. He knew where they were headed and it was not to a nearby school or even a nearby settlement. He had seen that type of crawler parked inside of a loading garage at the Chronopticus Network prison complex.

The waitress returned to their table and spoke up. "Isn't that sad? I just can't believe that many people could be troublemakers."

Pierce kept his facial expression blank while she took their drink order. In the dim lighting of the restaurant, the waitress' badge shone as if it were made of a bright white pearl. When she left, he activated a holographic menu on the tabletop. The menu rose up from the surface of their table and displayed all of the options in three dimensions. It also allowed him to rotate each dish before taking his order. His mood sank as many of the regular items appeared as empty plates. The remaining choices were healthy, but all he wanted tonight was a greasy cheeseburger, a side of zesty fries, and maybe a stout beer. Seeing none of those options, he ordered a plate of grilled teriyaki chicken and a side of rice pilaf.

Suzanne, who sat next to Pierce in the booth, leaned in and whispered into his ear. "I'm so glad you walked me out of work tonight."

"Why's that?"

"People were giving me grief today. And asking a lot of strange questions. Like what I did during my time in prison. Seems some of them had some neighbors taken away. Or maybe they turned their neighbors in, I don't know. I didn't tell them much other than I read a lot. When they asked me what books I told them non-fiction ones. When they asked me which ones, I mumbled and left the room and got some coffee."

Pierce could see by her downcast eyes that her response did not sit right with her. He whispered into her ear, "I don't know if I would have handled it any better."

Several minutes later their food arrived as more customers filed into the restaurant. Up on the wall telescreen an obnoxious announcer dressed in a black suit and a yellow, polka-dotted bowtie came onscreen. The words, "Time's up!" flashed above the man's head in a declaration of the end of the "High Noon" endeavor. Pierce glanced around and it was as if the patrons were oblivious to what was going on.

Somewhere in the distance, a whistle sounded.

"It's like a game show to them. Doesn't anybody understand what is happening?" Pierce said, raising his voice so it could be heard several tables away. The conversations in the nearby booths ceased and several people stared at him. In less than a minute they turned back to their own business as if nothing happened.

Before the waitress left their table again, Pierce asked her a question. "Do you happen to know where they are taking those people?" He pointed at the wall telescreen.

The waitress' eyes lit up. "I'm not really sure. But I think they get to participate in games."

"Games? I thought it was about the reeducation of troublemakers."

"It is. But don't worry. The games will be televised."

Pierce felt his stomach go into a slow churn. The scent of the rice nauseated him, but he did his best to pretend to enjoy the meal. Eventually, the waitress left.

"Pierce doesn't like his food," James said as he nibbled on a piece of cheese pizza.

Suzanne squeezed Pierce's thigh under the table. "Let's talk about this later."

"We have to get organized. Tonight," Pierce said under his breath.

She whispered into his ear. "We're outgunned."

"Nonsense. I have a plan."

Chapter Nine

As soon as Pierce returned home, he opened up the storage room. He pulled out several pieces of rocket scrap metal and other odds and ends he collected over the years and brought them into the living room piece by piece. He dug out a pair of metal springs and set them next to the sofa. He then walked over to his bookshelf and withdrew a book on medieval weaponry. Somehow he wished he could sit down with James and brainstorm ideas at this late hour.

Instead, he sat on the carpet and leafed through the book in search of ideas. The diagrams of catapults captivated him and the schematics of siege equipment stimulated him, but it was the comparison of crossbows that gave him hope. He pulled out a thin strip of metal and flexed it with his hands. He then laid this piece perpendicular to a short metal pole to gauge the feasibility of such a device.

Within an hour, with the help of a power drill and some other parts, he fashioned a makeshift crossbow. Due to a lack of a test site to fire his device, he pulled out one of the sofa cushions and propped it against the far wall in the living room. Then, he returned to the crossbow, propped it up on the coffee table, and strung it back with an aluminum pole as its payload.

With a sharp crack, the machine fired. It launched the pole through the cushion and into the wall.

After a few more hours of modification, he felt he had built a workable weapon. As the light of dawn broke through the slats on his living room window, he rubbed his eyes. He wondered what James could do with such a device. He stood up, brushed himself off, and went out for a walk.

As he left his home street, he ran into Kyrk, who again spoke gibberish to himself or whatever streetlight would listen. By now, Pierce figured the man had lost it or really was on to something important. They waved to each other. As Kyrk passed by, he pulled out a piece of paper, scribbled a furious note, and handed it to Pierce.

Pierce read the note in silence. The message said, "Did you hear about Pastor Capshaw? They found him last night. Put him on the telescreen this morning."

"That explains why I heard the whistle at dinnertime," Pierce said. He took a deep breath and shook his head. "It's like they're trying to take God out of the equation. Everywhere." He handed the paper back to Kyrk.

Kyrk scribbled another note and handed it back. It read, "They called it their biggest crusader catch. You think they're taking him to the prison?"

Pierce nodded. "So where is this Camp Io I hear about?" He said, deliberately raising his voice.

Kyrk's eyes widened. His badge was now a pale shade of orange. "Camp Io is the place to be. Everyone knows these endeavors won't last long once the rebellion really gets going."

Pierce smiled but still did not fully understand where Kyrk was going with his speeches. He wanted to discuss the crossbow he finished, but thought better of it.

The two of them looked toward downtown. The hands on the giant clock on the side of the City Center building remained frozen. A moment later, the video plate in Pierce's pocket rang out. He withdrew it and held it out in front of them. It was Suzanne.

The panicked expression on her face said it all. "Are you at home?"

"I'm out taking a walk. Is something wrong?"

"Go look at your telescreen. He's naming people. I'll hang up. Call me back."

In confusion, Pierce thought about walking back home, but instead let the call end and dialed up the Network news. On the screen, in mid-message, was Kalen again standing somewhere in downtown. In the distance and over his shoulder was the giant clock. Pierce scanned the neighborhood around them and then turned up the volume. Kyrk cringed.

"What is a hero to you?" Kalen said. "Is it someone who is courageous? Someone devoted? Someone that everyone looks up to? How well do you really know your heroes? Do you know them like I do?"

Pierce sighed.

Kalen continued. "In the spirit of entertainment, I want you to know who these people are too. That's why our next endeavor is called 'Countdown'. The clock you see behind me will be reset every twenty-four hours. During those twenty four hours a new person's history and their common routines will be announced."

Pierce and Kyrk gave each other a confused look.

"But here's a twist. I won't share their names. But can you figure out who they are? The reward for every turn-in during this endeavor is 75 food credits."

Pierce turned the video plate off and dropped it back into his pocket. "He just doesn't quit."

"Don't you want to see who the first contestants are?" Kyrk said.

"Not right now."

Kyrk withdrew his own video plate and held it out in front of him. He brought up Kalen's speech onscreen and this time it was Pierce who cringed.

"Our first two contestants saved you during the Great War. But are they really the heroes you've made them out to be? One is an accountant, but do you know what kind of an accountant he is? Back on Earth, he was known for cheating on exams, not paying his taxes, and gambling the night away. The other contestant is a chemical engineer who destroyed company property but now wants to push her beliefs on you at every turn. They are stuck in their ways and need our help. But where can you find them?"

Kalen grinned and continued. "I hear you can find a good accountant at the local casino. And the engineer? I hear Tranquility Merlot is on sale this week at the Magnopolis liquor store. But I digress. Just know this: a hero becomes a villain if you let them ramble on long enough."

At that, Pierce and Kyrk looked up from the video plate and stared at each other a moment.

"It's Ruelle Dorner, isn't it?" Pierce said.

Kyrk nodded. "I gotta go."

Pierce agreed and watched his friend run away at lightning speed.

Chapter Ten

Pierce stopped in at one of the city grocery stores and attempted to stock up on supplies. Although he knew his purchases were being logged somewhere in the Network, he figured if he picked up enough items over a long enough period of time their collective potential might go unnoticed. As he wandered through the aisles, many of the shelves were empty and prices on certain items were astronomical.

After he finished, he went to the checkout terminal. As he waited in line, a news headline scrolled on a nearby telescreen. It stated that Ruelle Dorner, her husband Ryan, and their daughter Jessie had been picked up on the outskirts of the city attempting to flee in a crawler vehicle. Pierce recalled how their badge colors were a deep shade of orange, which meant Kalen was working his way through the spectrum of threats. Yellow, he figured, was probably next on the hit list for a prison stay, or, as Kalen referred to it, reeducation.

Pierce was startled to see the footage of their capture. One shot showed Ruelle praying in what the news anchor called a "vain and confused plea for help". His mind was torn between silent anger and organized revolt. Despite working through the outcome of each scenario, none of the options brought him any peace.

As the checkout line moved forward, Pierce unloaded handheld lights, batteries for surface radios, antiseptic, and a bag of potatoes onto the conveyor belt. After he set all the items out, he realized how obvious it must have looked to the system what he had planned. As the belt pulled his items along and scanned them one by one he turned to look to see who was watching him.

"Didn't you used to be the mayor?" A perplexed voice said behind him. He bagged up his items and double-checked his badge color before he turned around.

He did not recognize the woman in line behind him. She looked to be in her early thirties and wore a white sweater that had musical notes printed on it. She held a bag of carrots in one hand and a loaf of bread in the other. He wondered how much of her income went to purchase those two items. He smiled to buy some time, but was unsure how much information he wanted to share. Finally, he replied, "Yes."

There appeared to be sincere compassion and concern in her eyes which disarmed him. "What happened?"

"I was replaced. Guess somebody had other plans for the city." All he wanted to do at this point was leave, and leave in a hurry. He stared at her badge. It was a deep orange.

"I would have kept you around," she said. "Things have gone nothing but downhill since the new mayor took over." She extended a hand to shake. "I'm Lynn, by the way. Omar Goldman's wife."

The tension in Pierce's shoulders dissipated. "It's nice to meet you. How is Omar these days?"

"He's worried about what's to come. What do you think?"

Pierce lowered his voice, leaned over, and whispered. "I think we need to make preparations." He motioned toward the supplies he just purchased. "Looks like we're in a time now where the heroes have been turned into villains and the villains are heroes. God help us."

At that moment, the lights in the store flickered. Pierce felt a shaking sensation under his feet that lasted ten seconds. A handful of candy bars tumbled off a nearby shelf and hit the floor.

"What was that?" Lynn asked.

"I don't know. It wasn't a rocket launch."

* * *

On his way back home, Pierce checked his video plate for the latest news feed coming out of the Network. The first story was that of a possible quake. No one knew its intensity since quake-measuring devices were not in use on the planet, yet the epicenter was east of the Magnopolis dome. No damage was reported, but nerves were rattled since settlers were told from day one that Mars had been volcanically dormant for thousands of years.

The next story talked about the reset of the giant clock in downtown. With rapt attention, he listened and tripped over the street curb several times in the process.

The reporter, a young man in his twenties with a heavy British accent, relished the moment as if it were a countdown on New Year's Eve. "Our next contestants are a couple from Magnopolis who never seem to pass up an opportunity to spew their hate speech. He was a guard and a software engineer who destroyed company property and frequently forgets dates and anniversaries. She has long black hair, brown eyes, and wants to start a music school in an attempt to indoctrinate your children. Our next countdown begins...now. As always, may the algorithms watch over you."

Pierce looked up. He could not see the downtown clock from here, but could only imagine what it looked like. He scanned his home street for any uptick in activity. Although he knew exactly who the next contestants were—Omar and Lynn Goldman—he wanted to warn them directly. Yet he knew that it was probably too late for that now. He wondered if his first and only encounter with Lynn would be his last.

As he reached his front door, he noticed Suzanne waiting on the front step. Her tired eyes and disheveled hair gave him the impression that she was not going to sleep well tonight.

She looked up. "Did you hear?"

"I just saw it. Know who I just ran into at the store tonight? Lynn. Omar's wife."

Suzanne put a hand to her open mouth. "Was this before or after you found out?"

"Before."

"Shouldn't we warn them?"

"It's too late for that. Besides, Omar's a news junkie. He'll know. And he's probably got a plan in place, too."

"Do you think we're next?"

Pierce knew that no matter what he said it would not quell her anxiety. He motioned toward the house and opened up the front door. "Here, come inside."

As it was, the living room was nearly impassible. Scrap metal, plastic, coils of wire, and tools covered the floor. He brushed some of it aside with his shoe.

Suzanne's eyes widened as she put her hands on her hips. "What are you planning to do with all of this?"

Pierce reached over alongside the sofa and pulled out the first of two crossbows. He held it out in front of them and then took aim at the telescreen wall.

"No! Don't!" She said as she turned away.

"I already did last night. I figure we got enough range with these to take out a few of the Cyclodes if they try to take us away."

"Pierce, no. I can't do this. I think we need to find a way out of here."

"What happens when we can't leave? I say we build more of these and raise an army."

"No. This doesn't feel right."

"I thought you said God was going to raise up people to fight."

Suzanne put both her hands on her temples. "I'm not sure. I don't know. Yes. But not like this."

"Don't you want to watch a demonstration?"

"No."

He loaded the bow and took aim at the sofa cushion against the wall again. "Are you sure? Last chance?"

"No."

She covered her eyes but peeled a hand back as he fired the bow. With a sharp pop, the arrow slammed through the cushion and into the wall.

"Think James could make it better?" Pierce said with a smile.

Suzanne dropped her hands and looked at the bow. "I know he can."

Chapter Eleven

The next day, Suzanne, James, and Pierce went out for a walk along Hilbert Curve near Pierce's home. Suddenly, Pierce heard a commotion coming from further down the street. It sounded like yet another street fight, and like the appearance of more and more of those as of late, he wanted nothing to do with it. This time he heard Omar Goldman's voice.

He stopped in the middle of the sidewalk and stood still. Before Suzanne could speak, he held up a hand and listened. He crept up alongside a nearby house. At odd intervals he peered around the corner to get a glimpse of the argument, while Suzanne and James remained behind him on the sidewalk.

On nearby Mandelbrot Curve, two third-generation Cyclode Sentinels stood around Omar and Lynn Goldman. One machine stood behind them with an ion coil pistol drawn and pointed at Omar's back, while the other machine stood in front and dictated instructions to them. Omar nodded but looked around as if he plotted a plan of escape in his mind. His wife shook with fear and shouted something to Omar in a language Pierce did not understand.

"All I'm asking for is evidence of the crime we committed. What are the charges?" Omar pleaded with the machine that stood before him.

Pierce dashed back past Suzanne. "Stay here. I'll be back." He ran full speed toward his house and once inside, he pulled out one of his crossbows with a handful of arrows. He slipped out of the house with the crossbow at his side.

He snuck in between a different set of houses and waved Suzanne and James over to his side. Once they arrived, and before Suzanne could object, he directed them to get down on the ground. He then crept up to the edge of one of the houses and took aim at the lead Cyclode. As he steadied his aim, he waited for the perfect moment to strike.

With a snap, the bow fired and a steel arrow lodged itself into a weak spot in the neck of the Cyclode's armor. Sparks flew and the machine was unable to turn its head in Pierce's direction.

Just as Pierce loaded up another arrow, the other machine fired in his direction and sent him running for cover. He waited a minute and then peered around the corner. He drew back the bow and fired again, this time at the back of the lead Cyclode's knee joint. The machine buckled on its left leg and fired a couple of ion coil rounds that slammed into the siding of a nearby house.

He drew back another arrow. By the time he looked around the corner, the rear machine fired back and knocked the bow out of Pierce's hands.

Omar and Lynn stood still in the street, although Pierce wanted to shout at them to run. After Pierce recovered, he started to walk toward the Cyclode Sentinel with the two arrows sticking out of it. The machine picked up on his approach and tried to turn toward him. Instead a few sparks and a cloud of smoke came out of its head.

"Sir," the machine said in its mechanized voice. "Step back. Do not approach. Do not…do not…"

"Why are you arresting my friends here?" Pierce said as he came within ten feet of them and put his hands on his hips. He observed that Omar and Lynn's badge colors were a solid orange.

"Step back. Do not approach." The machine's speech processors struggled which brought a smile to Omar's face.

"What have they done wrong? I think you've made a mistake."

"There is no mistake. These citizens have been deemed a threat. Please step back. Do not…do not…do not approach." The machine behind Omar continued to poke the ion coil pistol into the man's back as if to prod him to move forward.

"What if I told you I know of the location of Camp Io? Would you let them go then?" It was a gamble to even bring up the subject, Pierce decided, but if they were going to start systematically hauling people off, what did he have to lose?

Instead of responding to his question, the lead machine jerked and aimed its ion coil pistol directly at Pierce's chest. Pierce put up his hands. The machine snapped off the arrow in its neck and turned back toward Omar and Lynn and directed them to march into a nearby transport.

Omar and Lynn complied but pleaded with Pierce with their eyes. Pierce decided to march forward again since the lead Cyclode machine had taken its pistol off of him. As the second machine forced the couple into the open side door of the crawler, the first one again turned back toward Pierce and raised its pistol at him.

At this point, Pierce no longer cared what was going to happen. At worst, the pistol would probably only stun him, and in the confusion Lynn or Omar might be able to escape. He approached but after the couple was loaded into the crawler, the lead Cyclode lowered its weapon.

"Step back. You are not a threat for this endeavor."

"Oh, yes I am a threat. Look at my badge color." Pierce reached down and held out his badge at the machine but it did not respond. Confused, he turned the front of the badge back toward himself and noticed that its color had changed from orange to pure white.

He turned back toward the street behind him, where Suzanne remained on the ground. James had since moved up to the space between the houses, much like Pierce did, and held up a handheld device. He recognized it as the badge scrambler that James had toyed around with in the living room. By the time Pierce looked back toward the crawler, it pulled away and was heading toward one of the exits of the city.

He ran back to James, patted the boy on the back, and smiled. Together they walked back toward Suzanne who gave Pierce a burning stare that told him he had a lot of explaining to do.

"What were thinking over there?" She scolded him.

"I don't know what came over me."

"We need to pack."

Pierce nodded but inside wanted to organize a group to head out again to the Chronopticus prison complex instead.

Chapter Twelve

A few days later Pierce flipped on the Network news and nearly choked on the cinnamon roll he ate for breakfast. The lead story showed another parade of citizens in front of City Hall. Pierce could not tell if the event was being televised live or was shot at another time. In the lineup stood Ruelle Dorner, her husband, Ryan, and Omar and Lynn Goldman. All of them, along with many other citizens, stood statue-like and emotionless as if they were drugged. He puzzled over how they were all deemed to be a future threat since he knew Omar personally. He knew several other people were still on the wanted list as the countdown clock in the middle of downtown was reset and set spinning again with the details of another wanted citizen.

The news anchor, a young Malaysian woman with stern eyes, then came back onscreen and introduced an upcoming event that was to take place in the Coliseum. "Get ready citizens of Magnopolis and the surrounding settlements! In two days the Coliseum will be host to a series of games sponsored by the Dexler Corporation. Mayor Kalen Rusk says many of these games will be in the spirit of the Roman times with gladiator matches and never before seen animals on Mars."

It was then that the screen changed to an image of the redesigned interior of City Hall. He cringed as the camera panned through the mayor's office. Kalen had succeeded in turning the place into a pseudo-Roman palace with fake pillars and gold-leafed wallpaper. It was as if Kalen had suddenly declared himself emperor for life.

Pierce turned off the telescreen and dumped the rest of his cinnamon roll in the garbage. His food badge was now a tangerine color. He envisioned building more crossbows from the piles of scrap metal, plastic, and wire left on the living room floor. As he glanced over at the remaining crossbow on the sofa, he took a deep breath.

The previous bow only partially disabled the Cyclode and took too much time to load and aim. Without James' input there was no way he would be able to build a cache of weapons on his own. His own skills in weapons making were weak and James was in school during the day. He also needed more scrap anyway.

Compounding his dilemma, he still had yet to organize a resistance movement. Many of his potential candidates were now in prison. Multiple times over the past day he thought of ways he could have handled his confrontation with the Cyclodes differently, but in the end the outcome might have been the same. He knew that it was a matter of time before he and Suzanne were next on the list. He reached over to the end table and pulled out his hand-drawn maps of the settlements.

The Chinese, Indian, and Russian settlements were too far away and his knowledge of their governing styles was poor at best. His eyes locked in on one settlement: La Crescent. Known for its scientific and technological facilities, it looked like a better short-term choice that the risky drive to the Freeland settlement. Suzanne had visited the settlement once on a business trip and talked about it favorably. He circled the settlement on the map, plotted an escape route, and called Suzanne.

Chapter Thirteen

After James went to school, Pierce and Suzanne headed out to the La Crescent settlement, which was several miles south of Magnopolis. Suzanne drove her crawler out of the public dock and onto the highway which ran to the settlement. Pierce sat in the passenger seat and leafed through a copy of one of Gordyn Karst's notebook journals from Earth. He had secured copies of the journals before leaving Earth years ago, but never had a great deal of free time to sit down and go through them.

"Did you ever read these?" He asked Suzanne out of the blue.

"No. Anything useful in them?" She replied in a sarcastic voice.

"This guy was a pioneer. Of course there are useful things in here."

"To another engineer. Or an architect maybe." She gave him a smile.

"No. It's more than that. Besides all the diagrams and plans he took tons of notes. Notes about designs, testing, faith..."

"Faith?"

"Every once in a while he quotes the Bible." He flipped a page in the notebook. "He even wrote up a schedule about how often he read it and when he read each book." As Pierce scanned the page, he stopped at one particular diagram of a copper-colored spherical ship that Gordyn designed to fly in and out of thunderstorms. He had not seen a thunderstorm in many years now, and the only thing that resembled rain came out of the shower head in the bathroom.

Further down the page, a heading began with the words, "Eden Project". As he worked his way through the content he wondered if he should be reading it aloud to Suzanne.

"What?" She said as she looked over at him.

"How much do you know about the history of the Eden Project?"

"Not a lot. Kayla mentioned it when I was in prison. Why?"

"He's got an entry about it. Says here it was a project whose intent was to study human interaction and development in extreme environments. He was worried because some of the project founders were also interested in settling Mars. He thought they might be planning to bring all their ideas up here. Sort of like a big psychology experiment. Under the guise of space exploration, of course." He glanced over at her, but he could tell by the look in her eyes that the idea was not registering immediately.

"Says here his nephew, Steven Entner, was quite interested in it, too. Too interested. Know what else is odd?"

Suzanne tightened her grip on the steering wheel.

Pierce continued. "He says many of the founders were anti-God. Almost like they were all trying to escape this place."

"This place?"

"Earth."

He flipped another page and continued reading in silence to himself. Once he found a stopping point, he summarized what he just read to her. "And here it says the group involved architects, civil engineers, astronomers, electrical engineers, computer scientists, and get this...people who know how to work with gigantic data sets."

"So we're inside someone's simulation?"

He nodded and then stared out the front window of their crawler to watch the shifting rust-colored dunes roll ahead of them. A dust devil some fifty feet high whirled away at the foot of a nearby set of hills but did not move toward them. The road frequently was covered over by fine sand after periodic dust storms swept through the region. A mile ahead of them he could see a sand plow as it hurled aside mounds of fine dust. In the process it created a miniature dust storm of its own that gave the immediate surroundings a pale tan tinge. To the right, giant solar-cell arrays were spread out across the open ground to gather what meager sunlight came in.

He stared back down at the notebook and then read a warning that Gordyn had written in hasty script. "Interesting. He ends the entry with a warning about Entner. He says that he and his wife tried their best to steer him back toward faith but he thinks it's too late. Oh, and get this. Steven even wrote an essay for school titled, 'A World Without God'. He got an 'A' on it."

They sat for a minute in silence while Suzanne followed the snaking curves of the highway as it wound its way through the hills.

On the horizon the dark gray outline of the top of the La Crescent dome rose up like an alien moon. "What else did he write after that?"

"Not much in this book. I have some older ones here. But in this one it ends with an entry about him being nervous about an upcoming test flight of one of his experimental spherical craft. Says he was worried about it failing in extreme conditions. Then he talks about the upcoming test day and how some odd anomalies in the weather patterns made him think twice about what he was going to do."

"Is that the last entry?"

Pierce nodded his head. "Judging by the date, I think he ended up crashing the next day and it killed him."

* * *

By the time they arrived at the crawler dock on the edge of the La Crescent settlement dome, Pierce could already tell this place was different from Magnopolis. Near the northern fringes of the domed city, solar panels turned like flowers with the sun and tall, looming, factory-like buildings with smokestacks pushed steam into the atmosphere. Although Pierce had heard there were scrubbers built into the smokestacks, he wondered what the region would look like in a year's time if enough pollution was dumped into the sky.

Construction on this particular settlement dome started a few months after Magnopolis was finished and new design patterns had been incorporated early on in the process. Although this dome used panels that could be made transparent during the light of midday, the panels also doubled as solar collectors. As the crawler bay doors opened before them, he found the lighting here was warmer, the airlocks were improved, and the arrival process was fully automated. The parking bays were also underground and beneath the edge of the city.

After Suzanne parked their vehicle, the airlock doors closed behind them. Pierce set Gordyn's notebook in the backseat and glanced at the crossbow he packed for the trip.

Suzanne looked back and gave him a cold stare. "Why did you bring that?"

"Just in case."

With a sigh, she exited the crawler.

He left the bow in the backseat but hoped it would not be a decision he would regret. After leaving their crawler behind, they passed through another set of airlocks and into the city.

Inside, Pierce felt as if he had stepped into a higher tech version of Magnopolis. Here, the streets were paved in bluish-gray rock, and although the neighborhood homes had the same type of fake grass as his neighborhood, the grass looked healthier here. In several of the backyards, tall, yellow, sunflower-shaped lamps emitted a cool purple light. The lamps sat atop metal poles that pointed down toward backyard gardens.

As they walked down the block, he did not see any busybees hovering above them and perhaps there was no need for them here. He did not see any of the curbside tracking devices like he saw back in Magnopolis, but it was possible the sensors were embedded in the road beneath their feet. From his vantage point it appeared as if all the roads were laid out in a spoke pattern that fed into the center of the city. High above, each streetlight they passed beneath emitted a disc of soft light that only appeared when they stood underneath the lamp.

In the middle of the city, a group of identical multi-story buildings formed a circle. The sides of the buildings were covered in white and pale blue lines that made them look as if they were wrapped in graph paper. Their vertical edges emitted a soft, neon glow. Atop each building was a statue of a human figure that held up a symbol. One figure held up a large-toothed gear, while another held up an old-fashioned model of an atom. Another figure held up a chemistry flask. The circular buildings were several feet shorter than the central building, which had its own human statue on top. That statue held up a white, orange, blue, and rust-colored orb on its shoulders as if it were a statue of Atlas holding up Mars instead.

There was a sterile, automated feel to the city as if it was devoid of human activity. Pierce could see a handful of people moving about on the streets ahead and on either side of them, but he did not see any vehicles here. He also did not see any Cyclode Sentinel machines. He turned to Suzanne as they continued to move toward the center of the city. "What do they do for enforcement around here?"

As they passed by a clothing store, a voice emanated from an electronic display on the side of the building. "Good day, sir," the voice said. "Would you be interested in seeing our select line of business suits custom-tailored to you?"

"No," Pierce replied, not thinking that he was talking to a machine.

"Sir, what about your wife? Perhaps she would be interested in our latest line of sweaters. Perfect for gazing at the stars…"

"We're not interested," Suzanne said, joining in on the fun.

"How about a new pair of shoes? This week, imported from Earth…"

"How about umbrellas?" Pierce said. "I miss umbrellas and walking in the rain. Do you have any umbrellas? Can you make it rain?"

The display hesitated. "I'm sorry, sir. We do not carry umbrellas. We do not carry rain."

"What about snow boots? Do you have those?" Suzanne said with a smile.

"I'm sorry. We do not carry snow boots."

"Well, what do you carry?"

The display sat in silence for a minute. "Would you be interested in seeing our select line of business suits custom-tailored to you?"

Pierce and Suzanne walked on, but the electronic display continued to have a conversation with itself. Suzanne pointed at a warehouse that had a fenced-in yard attached to the back of it. Inside of the yard two men, both wearing olive-colored, long-sleeve shirts and khakis, stood around a remote-controlled machine. One of the men circled around the machine, which resembled a male lion. The machine had four legs, a jointed tail, a mane made of hundreds of brass-colored plates, and a fearsome set of teeth. Pierce motioned for Suzanne to move further up the street to get a closer look.

They hid behind another warehouse building across from the yard. The two men surrounding the lion backed up as if to give the machine room to maneuver. At the press of a button, the lion stood up on all fours and began to march in a slow circle. One of the men then propped up a black plastic cutout of a human in front of the machine. The mechanical lion circled around the cutout with algorithmic precision and without warning pounced on it and pressed it to the ground. The cutout crunched and cracked into several pieces under the weight of the machine.

"Isn't there supposed to be some kind of event at the Coliseum tomorrow?" Suzanne said.

Pierce nodded. "It's supposed to be the first event with the citizens they picked up off the streets. I think we should pay a visit," he said after a pause.

"But how? We can't get in there with our badges the way they are."

"Sure we can. We'll just need a little help from James."

"Just leave your crossbow at home."

"Let's get out here. I have a bad feeling about the lion and this place."

"I was wondering when you were going to say that."

As they walked back toward the crawler dock, they passed what at first appeared to be an empty lot. When Pierce moved forward, the walls of the building appeared next to him as if they were painted with some type of cloaking material. He stepped back as Suzanne gave him a bewildered look.

"Back up," he said.

She moved back and stood next to him. The building disappeared. When they lurched forward, it reappeared.

"How would you like to work at a company that disappears every time you left for the day?" He said.

"Some days, I wouldn't mind it all."

They continued toward the exit. Despite his reservations about the place, he tried to take in as many sights as he could. Near the crawler dock entrance they passed a tree with dark green, star-shaped leaves. The tree held orange and purple apple-shaped fruit.

Suzanne stopped in front of the tree to stare. "What is this?"

"I'm a pepperfruit tree, Ms. Entner," the tree said in a deep male voice.

Suzanne shot a sharp glance at Pierce. She looked over at Pierce's food badge and then at her own. "What's a pepperfruit and how'd you know my name?"

"Ms. Entner, a pepperfruit is a cross between an apple and several varieties of pepper. The taste resembles a spicy apple. I know your name because it is listed in the Network Archives," the tree replied.

Pierce debated whether or not he should pull a piece of fruit off the tree to count its seeds. Then he wondered if the tree would scream. Thinking better of it, he tugged at Suzanne's shirt and pulled her toward the exit.

The walls near the crawler airlock were plastered with more Dove League posters. Above the airlock, an electronic sign changed its message to read: "Thank you for visiting the City of Man, Pierce and Suzanne. Come again and may the algorithms watch over you."

Chapter Fourteen

Game day came to the Magnopolis Coliseum with a blend of showbiz, pomp, and dread. Pierce and Suzanne walked up Cantor Street toward the ticketing gate of the stadium, each carrying a short range version of James' badge scrambler. Through openings in the stone arches around the perimeter of the stadium, Pierce caught a glimpse of the crowds gathered together in the stands. Although he did not know the exact seating capacity of the place, he knew there were hundreds, maybe even a thousand gathered and he knew everything was being televised. He wondered how well this event would be received by those travelling inbound from Earth and whether they would want to turn around and head back for home the moment they found out.

He held Suzanne's hand tight. "If they're going to throw people to mechanical lions, do you think they're going to give them anything to fight back with?"

"You mean like a sword?"

"Anything. Wits only get you so far with something that can outrun you at every turn." Uneasiness settled into his stomach, almost like the time when he was mayor and found out via the telescreen that his life was being threatened. He looked down at his badge and noticed it was still a solid tangerine color. He reached into his pocket and activated the badge scrambler James created. He watched as his badge color transformed into an ivory white. He pointed to his badge. "Almost forgot."

Suzanne nodded and clicked on her badge scrambler. She took a deep breath and squeezed his hand tight.

As they entered the Coliseum, a man in a slate-blue uniform checked their badges and let them pass. Pierce felt his pulse accelerate as they moved toward the stairways that ran up into stands on either side of them. The Coliseum was built in a semi-circular shape, with the arc opening up toward downtown, which, if set in a city back on Earth, might have been a more scenic view with the sky as a backdrop. Here, the static view of the city's dome gave the scene an artificial look as if it were taking place entirely on a movie set.

As they scaled the stairs to the right, he felt as if everyone they passed stared at them and subsequently whispered to one another afterward. When they finally found a pair of seats, they sat down. The stands were made of a dull Martian concrete with flecks of gray and olivine scattered throughout the rust-colored stone.

Pierce then stared out at the crowd and recognized several faces. He drew a breath of relief when he realized they were too far away to approach him. Several sections over, he spotted Midori, a Japanese woman whom he worked with to take down Io. At the moment she was looking away, but had a solemn look on her face. Before she could catch sight of his eyes he turned away and looked at Suzanne.

"What did you mean a while back when you said God would raise up people to deal with this situation? I know you said I would lead them but when I look out on the crowd all I see is a sea of white badges. I've never seen so many." His voice trailed off.

"That's the response I got when I prayed. I don't know anything else beyond that. I'm sorry."

"And now Kalen's pitting us against one another. One thing you never explained to me was how you went from fighting me about my faith to joining me in it. I know what you said before about things happening to you while you were in prison and all that. And I know that you've been reading the books I lent to you."

She withdrew her hand from his. A part of him wished he would have rephrased what he just said and another part of him was frustrated and needed answers. He felt beads of sweat form around his shirt collar.

"Don't you trust me?" She said.

"Sure I trust you."

"You don't sound like you mean it."

Pierce closed his eyes and leaned his head back. He recalled the first time he walked with her through the ruins of Magnopolis and how he doubted whether he could trust what she said to him. Times had changed, but his own insecurities sometimes got the best of him. He felt the muscles in the back of his neck tighten up. "I do mean it.

It's just..."

"You don't know who to trust anymore."

"Right. If you look over to your right a few sections you'll see what I mean. Midori is up there. I thought I saw Reed, too. Both have pure white badges on. I don't know if I could trust anybody I used to work with on the City Council either. Far as I know they're all still employed and I'm the only one who's been thrown out."

Suzanne cleared her throat. She crossed her arms and rested them on her knees. She then put her head on her arms and stared at him. "When I was growing up we went to church once in a while. I didn't really understand what was going on half the time, why they had all these rituals, and why we went. I tried getting along with some other kids but every time I talked about my family they shut down on me. I felt unwanted. Eventually my Mom stopped taking me and we never went back."

"Was that the year you lost your dad?"

"It was. Guess it was a last ditch effort by Mom to try to make sense of things. As time went on I kept surrounding myself with things to back up my beliefs. Or lack of them. I read books and kept friends like that too. I put up walls everywhere. God, I put up a lot of walls."

A moment of silence opened up between them and Pierce stepped into it. "Until you met me."

She grinned. "Maybe. I still have walls up. But I'm working on it. Or God's working on it. Can't say I'm always agreeing to it. But at least a lot of the loneliness is gone."

A male voice boomed over the loudspeakers that circled the arena below. "Welcome all to the First Annual Magnopolis Games. Today's contests will feature recent contestants in the Countdown and High Noon endeavors. This also ends endeavor two. Or, as we like to say in the business, time's up!"

A nervous wave of laughter swept through the crowd. It was followed by a smattering of applause.

Pierce shot Suzanne a startled look. "Does this mean there's another endeavor on the way?"

The announcer barreled ahead. "Our first contestants feature two engineers and their partners as they do battle in the arena." A ripple of gasps travelled through the crowd.

Pierce eyed the entrance gate on one side of the arena. The entrance was covered by a steel grate which split in two as both halves retreated into the arena wall. A Cyclode Sentinel forced the four contestants into the middle of the playing field, which was covered in sand and overlaid with a laser-generated grid of hexagons. The hexagons radiated a fiery bright blue aura. Some of the hexagons contained red cloth flags on metal poles which were attached to a circular base to keep them upright.

The announcer broke in again. "The goal of this first contest is for the contestants to work together as a team in order to capture as many flags as possible. But look out! Danger waits at every turn when the mechanical lions are released!"

Another gasp went through the crowd.

The four contestants moved out into the playing field and then separated into pairs. Each contestant was equipped with a short sword whose blade was no longer than Pierce's forearm and a heavy shield that reduced mobility. Pierce felt his shoulders tighten up even more when he recognized who they were. He leaned over to whisper in Suzanne's ear. "Look. It's Omar and his wife. And Ruelle. And Ryan. I wonder if they're using the lions we saw back at La Crescent."

Omar moved cautiously toward one of the red flags and gave directions to his wife. None of them wore any protective gear except for a basic breastplate which sat on their shoulders and looked to be made of paper-thin aluminum. All four of the contestants kept their eyes on the first lion that emerged, which was soon followed by another. Each lion had a mane made of metal, as if it were a protective shield for its neck. The lions were just like the ones Pierce saw back in La Crescent, but their manes resembled an array of knives in this light. Their bodies were shaped like lions back on Earth and their eyes glowed with an eerie golden aura. The tail on the lead animal swished back and forth in a jointed serpentine motion.

Omar reached out and tore one of the flags off of its pole. At the same time, the lead lion charged and leapt at his outstretched hand. With a slashing arc Omar took a slice at the lion's head but the machine only took a glancing blow. The lion backed off a step and allowed Omar to pocket the flag before charging again. In the meantime, Lynn darted over a few hexagons and ripped another flag from its pole. In haste, she tucked the flag into a pocket in her pants.

Ruelle and Ryan zeroed in together on a flag of their own and watched as the other lion tried to cut them off. The lion appeared to be programmed differently, as if it ran on altered algorithms, despite having an identical appearance. As Ruelle grasped one of the flags, Ryan stabbed at the lion just behind the shoulders. Sparks flew as the machine reeled and was knocked onto its side. A puff of smoke rose up from the machine as a gasp went through the crowd.

Ryan took another swing at the machine but as the blow fell, the machine writhed out of the way and scrambled back onto all fours to regroup. It scampered back several paces before it sized the couple up again from a different angle.

Pierce shifted his eyes from the action in the arena back up into the stands and watched both Reed and Midori as they sat together in the crowd. Reed looked uncomfortable and more than once put a his hand to his eyes. In contrast, Midori clenched her fists as the lions took alternating shots at the participants below.

As Omar and Lynn worked to pick up another flag, Pierce noticed a potential danger in their strategy. He fought the urge to rise to his feet and yell out instructions to them and instead gripped the seat even tighter.

Then, in a moment he felt coming ever since the match started, Pierce watched in shock as the tail on one of the lions swung around and smacked into Lynn's right leg. The tail then swung around and hit her in the side and knocked her off of her feet. As she dropped to the arena floor, the crowd went silent and many rose to their feet.

From this height, Pierce could not see Lynn move at all. It reminded him of a boxing match he saw on television as a kid where one fighter knocked out the other, but the downed opponent left on a stretcher, only to die later at a nearby hospital.

Pierce and Suzanne rose to their feet, and the color drained out of Suzanne's face. She put a hand first to her eyes and then her mouth. A tear rolled down her cheek. Pierce's shock soon turned to anger. He felt Suzanne restrain him as he started to march toward the aisle.

Below, Omar sprinted over to his wounded wife with his sword in hand. Along the way he swung wildly at the lion that injured her. He struck so many blows at the lion's head that the machine crumpled to the arena floor in a heap of sparks and metallic groans. He then drove the sword into the lion's head, effectively killing its circuitry. The lion thrashed about in the sand with the sword stuck in its eye until the golden light in the other eye went out. The machine seized up and belched out a final puff of white smoke like a flag of surrender.

A moment later he reached his wife. Ryan ran over, too, while Ruelle guarded their backsides from the remaining lion. As Omar knelt down next to his helpless wife, Ryan reached down and placed his hands first on her side and then on her leg. He closed his eyes and looked toward the roof of the arena and prayed.

Pierce tried to read his lips. Ryan pled with God for her healing. As he looked over again at Midori and Reed, he noticed Reed had already left and Midori looked remorseful. As several people stood in silence, others filed out of the stands to leave.

Suzanne spoke up. "I'm getting sick to my stomach. Can we leave?"

"I agree. We gotta get out of here."

Just then, Pierce noticed that Lynn began to move on the arena floor. The crowd made a collective sigh of relief, mixed with occasional jeers. Omar flung his breastplate armor aside and tore off his shirt to tie a tourniquet around her leg. Blood began to seep out onto the arena floor and as Omar secured the tourniquet, she sat up and said something to him. It was then Pierce realized the purpose of the sand in the arena was to soak up blood.

Ryan and Omar both had shocked expressions on their faces as she motioned to them to help her up. She put her arm around her husband and stood up on her feet, despite Omar warning her to lay down.

Suzanne pulled on Pierce's shirt. Her eyes were full of tears and worry. "Let's go now."

Pierce nodded. The other lion circled about and lunged at Ruelle. Ryan slashed at the creature with furious abandon and Ruelle soon joined in. Together they slammed the lion to the ground until it, too, fell into a jumbled, smoking heap. A small cheer came out from the crowd as the announcer took over again.

Out of the corner of his eye, Pierce noticed a dark, curly-haired figure midway up in the stands. For an instant, he turned his head to look, but wished he did not. It was Kalen Rusk, relishing the moment, while surrounded by security guards. Kalen made eye contact with Pierce and Pierce returned a fierce glare before turning away.

The contestants soon left the arena. Just as Pierce and Suzanne descended the stairs toward the exit, four more contestants were announced and Pierce had to look back. There, Pastor Capshaw and Artelius Gray were paraded out onto the arena floor along with two others. Pierce suspected neither the pastor nor Artelius were capable with a short sword.

Two new lions charged out of the gate full speed and before either the pastor or the jeweler could react, one of the lions made a pass at both of the men. The two men toppled to the ground while a third lion thundered out of the gate. Artelius did not move until his arms twitched. Pierce and Suzanne pushed their way out of the stadium. As they returned onto the street the crowd roared, then gasped. Pierce knew what was about to happen next.

The scream that followed came from Pastor Capshaw.

Chapter Fifteen

The walk to Lisabeth's house was a silent one, although Pierce knew Suzanne shared both his anger and apprehension over what they just witnessed. He assumed that Pastor Capshaw and Artelius were as good as dead, the latter probably having suffered a heart attack. He heard a busybee follow them all the way from the Coliseum and a part of him wanted to knock the thing out of the sky.

"Still think the crossbow idea went too far?" Pierce said.

Suzanne did not reply but she did offer a smile. As they arrived at her sister's house, Lisabeth opened the door. She had a mournful look in her eyes, as if she knew what had happened. When they stepped inside, James was waiting for them on the sofa, reading a book.

James jumped up and ran over to his mother's side. He bear-hugged her leg.

Lisabeth said, "So how did it go?"

Pierce nodded but chose his words carefully. "Not the way we expected."

"What happened?" James said with excitement in his voice.

Suzanne looked to the side, but Pierce pressed on. He knelt down next to James. "It was just a game. I wouldn't go see it again, though."

"What kind of game?"

"A game of man versus machine."

"Who won?"

"The people did."

The excitement in James' eyes faded and Pierce could not resist giving the boy a hug. In his heart, he knew he would lay down his life for the boy and his mother but there was no sufficient way of expressing this thought.

The three of them soon left for Pierce's house. On the way back, Kyrk walked alone along a nearby street holding a video plate in one hand. Today, Kyrk barked at someone on the video plate before he tucked the device into his pocket. He uttered the words "Camp Io" again with a fierce look of determination.

"There he goes with the Camp Io thing again," Pierce said. He whispered into her ear. "What I want to know is why we haven't been picked up yet. Why hasn't Kyrk been picked up?"

"Be careful what you wish for."

Up ahead on the street, just a block over from City Hall, Pierce spied the faint outline of a trap door that was cut into the pavement. He paced up to it and then knelt down.

"What is it?" She said.

He felt along the pavement and let his fingers trace out the edge of the escape door which led to a tunnel that ran back into City Hall and next to his old office. "They say there is more than one tunnel under these streets. Some are for maintenance, but I think some others are for escape."

"What are you thinking?"

Pierce let his fingers slip into a narrow notch in the door and he heaved it up with a single motion. The door opened to a dimly lit tunnel beneath the road. "I think we should do some exploring while there's time."

James gasped as he peered inside. "Can we go in there? I wanna see."

"I wonder if these tunnels hook up with any of the other settlements. Shall we check it out James?"

After Pierce lifted the door up, he started down the concrete stairs that ran underneath the road. He motioned for them to follow.

Suzanne let James go first. Pierce withdrew a small flashlight from his pocket and led the way through the tunnel to a point halfway between the door and City Hall. There, a passage branched off to the right. He led the way down the unexplored passage and stopped about fifty feet into it.

"What is it?" Suzanne asked.

He swept his flashlight down two more passages which opened up to the right and to the left of them. "More tunnels. We may have to make a map of these at some point. Rumor had it that this passage to the right may even lead to La Crescent."

"Why would you want to go back there?"

"I don't. But it might buy us time until we come up with something better."

In the distance, Pierce heard what sounded like footsteps. He motioned for them to go back through the way they came. "Apparently, we're not the only ones looking around down here."

Just as they were about to ascend the steps leading back to the street, the ground rumbled beneath their feet. This time the shaking lasted twenty seconds and shook dust down into their eyes.

Pierce gripped James' hand and led him up the stairs. Suzanne followed until they were back on the street again. He closed the trap door but did not see any damage in their immediate area.

"Was that another quake?" Suzanne asked.

Pierce nodded. "The settlements are built between mountain ranges. Volcanic ones to be exact."

Chapter Sixteen

Pierce sat at his kitchen table digging though the remainder of Gordyn's notebooks. Along with numerous diagrams of fantastic flying machines that were never built, each notebook held more clues as to the real nature of the elusive Eden Project. Early potential settlement candidate testing was planned to be rigorous, extensive, and somewhat controversial. It went beyond stressing a candidate's physical, mental, and emotional abilities. Granted, there were the usual battery of background checks, educational requirements, and checks for mental illness that would have weeded out many of the candidates before they even reached the physical testing stage. Gordyn also noted there were public arguments about whether the high standards set for the psychological tests could be offset by a person's physical abilities, although there was little evidence of the final outcome of those discussions.

As he turned the page, he found a copy of an early set of test results for one of the potential candidates. There was no explanation as to how Gordyn got a hold of such a document, other than maybe having an inside source that he never disclosed. The document was filled with graphs and charts and listed a basic personality summary, but did not give a hint as to what questions were asked.

Near the end of the document, he found some notes about the candidate and how they were recommended for a possible flight to Mars. The notable point in the summary was that the candidate had "no known religious affiliation". Throughout this particular notebook, Gordyn commented more than once that there was a distinct bias in picking people without any faith or religious belief system at all, at least in the initial stages.

As Pierce thought about this a moment, he recalled reading an autobiography from John Winslow where the same issue was brought up. Winslow and his wife were among the first settlers of Galetown on Mars. Winslow said he and his wife felt like a novelty on the Mars mission for their religious beliefs or that they were added at the last minute as a way of appeasing an element of believers back on Earth. The original two candidates were eliminated at the very end for two different reasons: one broke their leg in a mountain climbing accident and would miss the flight window altogether while the other picked up mononucleosis and risked infecting others on the mission due to the close nature of the quarters on the flight out to Mars.

Winslow also warned about possible future outcomes of a drive to eliminate all faith systems from the settlements of Mars. Although his narrative did not explicitly state that such a process was underway, it was clear what direction Dexler Corporation was heading with things. Kalen Rusk's takeover over the Magnopolis government only cemented these developments and Pierce wondered what he could due to keep the carnage from getting worse. It seemed the Eden Project was built on the premise of colonizing a new world without any reference to God anywhere in the culture. In some respects, the more he thought about it, the more it seemed like a giant psychological experiment by Steven Entner and others at Dexler Corporation's expense.

All this research made Pierce feel like he was suffocating here. The walls in the kitchen seemed to close in now and he felt a bit dizzy. He leaned back in his chair and took a drink of water.

He walked back out to the living room and surveyed the remainder of his scrap metal supply. If they could not get a rocket flight out of here, and Kalen was eventually going to haul them in, it would not be without a fight.

He searched around the room for ideas. He walked over to his beloved bookcase and sighed. *What good are these books anyway*, he thought, *if I'm not around to read them*? He tore all of the books off the shelf and pulled the bookcase down to the floor. He dragged it over by the sofa and searched around for his hammer and screwdriver.

Then, the front door buzzer rang. He ambled over to the door to find Suzanne holding a video plate, which she then held out to him.

"What did you find?" He asked, somehow not wanting to know the answer.

"See for yourself. I got a hold of a few versions of the new arrival questionnaires. You know, the ones they ask you in the beginning of the process and the ones they ask after someone's stayed here a few months."

"And?" Pierce flicked his thumb across the video plate screen and scanned through one of the early applicant questionnaires.

"They ask a lot of religious questions. I'd be surprised if they weren't running into legal trouble back on Earth because of it, but we are on a different planet." There was a mournful ending to her sentence as if she was beginning to second guess their existence here.

He looked up from the video plate and into her eyes. "Ever get the feeling it's time to go back home?"

A wave of relief washed across her features. "I was beginning to think I was the only one who felt that way."

"No. I've thought about it lately. If we can't get a group together to take care of this problem, I don't know what other options we have."

"You're not thinking of a violent overthrow are you?"

He did not reply. Instead, he looked back over at his toppled bookcase in the middle of the living room floor.

She took the video plate back from him and changed screens. "Did you see this?" She held the plate back out to him so he could read the news headline. It stated that the shaking they felt in the tunnel was caused by yet another quake in a similar location as the previous one.

"I hope they figure out where the fault line is. And fast," he said. He took the plate from her again and scrolled through the article. He returned to the main news page only to find a picture of himself next to one of Suzanne. "Oh, look, we're in the news."

Suzanne leaned over and stared hard at the images. She read the headline aloud. "Endeavor number three has just been announced by the mayor."

"But I'm not the mayor. So why'd they use our pictures?"

"Because the name of the endeavor is Steadman's Run."

Chapter Seventeen

Pierce took back the video plate and read the article that detailed the endeavor aloud. The rules for this endeavor were to hunt and track down those with yellow badges, along with others who were not included in previous endeavors, which included Suzanne and him. He recalled how the crowd at the Coliseum sported predominantly white badges with a smattering of yellow badges here and there. This fact alone made him thankful for James' badge scrambler, which made him wonder if anybody from the day at the Coliseum put his face together with today's article.

The article also showed a picture of Kalen Rusk wearing a bizarre outfit in public and on the day of the games. The outfit consisted of a gold-colored breastplate, a gold-trimmed black shirt, a vermillion cape, a leather belt with alternating black and vermillion leather strips hanging down, and brown sandals. From the tone of the article Pierce wondered if Kalen was taking things to a point beyond where anybody else wanted to go.

As he flipped his way through the day's news, he also noticed another piece about how the military was growing under Kalen's leadership. Although he could not quite fathom the need for a military infrastructure for Magnopolis, one could not get far in the settlements without coming across an increasing Russian, Indian, and Chinese presence since they established bases here a few years ago. Perhaps the move was looking toward the future and trying to prevent what some may see as an inevitable outcome once the issues of water supplies began to rear up, but who knew. So far as he knew, no missiles were pointed in their direction.

"I don't suppose you saw what was put in downtown, did you?" Suzanne asked, her voice heavy with unease.

"Beyond the giant clock on the City Center building?"

"Now they have a giant hourglass in Meres Park. Here, let me pull up a picture for you." She took the video plate back out of his hands and scrolled through some images. She held it out to him with a frown. There was weariness in her eyes he had not seen before.

"Give me a break. What's that thing filled with? Red sand? Has the sand started pouring yet?"

"It won't until six o'clock tonight."

He looked over at a nearby wall clock. "That gives us a few hours to work with. Now I'm thinking we should plan our escape route out of here."

"I thought you wanted to fight."

"You mean you thought about what I said earlier?"

"I've been thinking about it a lot. What are we running from? Maybe this is the way we're supposed to go out. As martyrs in the New World. Our friends are getting taken away. Now that we know what's happening, shouldn't we try to stop it from the outside? Before we lose even more mobility?"

The thought of being incarcerated had been a remote one for him up until this moment. "What are they going to announce at six o'clock by the way?"

"How to find us. Which shouldn't be hard. You were a public figure and still are to some people. I know people at work who believe you were wronged and see you as a hero of sorts."

"But will they come to our defense? What if they get hauled away for helping us? I haven't heard anything about any street battles or people trying to save their friends and family. But maybe after what happened at the Coliseum people are going to start waking up."

They both eyed each other. The more he wrestled with such thoughts, the more he felt the neighborhood and the walls of his own house closing in on him and Suzanne. A myriad of questions raced through his mind. What would happen to James? As far as he knew James' badge was a faint yellow color that could pass for white in the right light. Or was he using a badge scrambler wherever he went? Was Lisabeth even safe? She kept her personal beliefs close and despite multiple conversations on the subject over the years with her, he was never quite sure where she stood.

He continued. "Maybe we should come up with a list of people we can trust first. Or can't. Then figure out our escape route. Here, come inside."

She crossed her arms and shivered. "I don't have a good feeling about any of this."

"Me either. But I'll start." Back in the living room, he pulled out a sheet of notebook paper from a nearby desk drawer. He drew a line down the middle of the page and split it into two columns. He started writing in the leftmost column. The first name he wrote down was "Lisabeth."

"Which list is she on?" Suzanne said.

"People we can trust."

She let out a deep sigh. "She has a white badge. She's also been clamming up lately about her beliefs. I can't get her talking about any of them even though this is all over the news. I know where she used to stand, but now I don't know."

Pierce wrote her name on the right side of the paper but did not erase her name from the left side. He felt like he was employing some sort of crude sorting algorithm, an operation that the Chronopticus Network and its battery of powerful servers performed in milliseconds. He thought about the co-workers who used to sit with him on the City Council and wrote their names on the right side. Next, thoughts of seeing Reed and Midori in the stands surfaced in his mind. He wrote Reed's name in the left column.

"Are you sure about him?" Suzanne asked.

"He helped with some investigations in past. I talked with him again at the casino the other week. Remember? I also saw him at the games the other day."

"So wouldn't he belong on the other side of the page?"

"As soon as the games got violent and Lynn fell, he got up and left in disgust. I could see it in his face. As for Midori..." He wrote her name on the right side, but had the urge to rearrange that choice. "I'm not sure where her loyalty lies. She claims to be all in for the company, but I think there's a struggle going on."

As they worked through the list of people they knew, both co-workers and friends, the uneasy feeling in Pierce's mind only intensified. He could not decide if he wanted to check the news reports in a few minutes to try and predict his own demise. There was something morbid about watching your own death sentence being pronounced on the wall telescreen, although he had his fill of death threats when he was mayor.

Pierce pulled out another piece of paper along with the crude paper maps of the settlements he made the other day. Together they sketched out their plan of escape, listing all the possible exit routes including the location of their crawler vehicles, how long it would take to reach them on foot, and the location of the tunnels they discovered under the streets.

"When does James come home from school?" He said as he tucked the list of divided names into his pants pocket.

"He'll be home within the hour. God, he must be so scared by now."

"Let's pick him up at your place and head to Lisabeth's."

"We won't be safe there after six."

"We might be if she doesn't answer the door."

He ran into his bedroom and pulled out a backpack from the closet. He shoved two shirts and a pair of pants inside. Underwear and socks came next. Back in the living room he packed up the maps and then remembered his notebook full of future city plans. With a momentary sadness, he crammed the notebook inside.

He returned to Suzanne's side. "You ready? Let's go."

Suzanne reached over onto the sofa. She pulled out the last remaining crossbow Pierce built. "Now I'm ready."

Chapter Eighteen

That night at Lisabeth's house they sat around a table in the living room discussing their potential plans while James slept in bed. Lisabeth kept the house lighting to a minimum in order to discourage visitors from knocking on her door. In front of them on the table were paper maps that illustrated possible escape routes, tunnels, and the time needed to accomplish each plan. Pierce felt a headache coming on, but he knew their flight might have to take place at any minute.

He was sure people had already checked out his house and Suzanne's house hours ago. For all he knew, people were still checking on their houses into all hours of the night. Fortunately, the last news bulletin about "Steadman's Run" was woefully lacking in information compared to the location probabilities that were given about the other people in the other endeavors. The bulletin gave Pierce Steadman an eighteen percent chance of being at the Magnopolis Library, which was now closed for the night. Suzanne was given a forty-two percent chance of being at her job, which she quit hours ago without notifying anybody at the company.

Their backpacks sat next to the back door. Although Lisabeth continually reassured them about their safety and that she would never give away their location, Pierce had seen financial incentives and rewards for each endeavor affect people in unpredictable ways. He tried to study her facial expressions without being too obvious about it. Eventually, he turned his attention back to the map in front of them.

"I'm thinking we could hit this outer tunnel entrance sometime tonight. Maybe stash our belongings there, or just head down below. It's probably not monitored anyway and the busybees would have an impossible time visually tracking anything in the darkness down there." He looked up to Suzanne to see if the idea registered with her approval. She nodded.

He pressed on. "I'm thinking if we could get to your crawler in the dock, then we could head out to the Freeland settlement. I may have a couple of contacts there I could rely on. Then I was thinking..."

There came a knock at the front door.

All three of them looked up. Lisabeth motioned for Pierce and Suzanne to head into the kitchen to buy time. She stood up, pressed the creases out of her blouse, and paced slowly up to the door. She looked through the eyehole on the door while Pierce peered from around the corner in the darkened kitchen.

The front door slid open to reveal a man in his twenties, dressed in a baggy white shirt and blue jeans, standing there with his thumbs in the belt loops of his pants. The evening light of the dome shone across the floor and just reached the edge of the kitchen. The man slurred his speech, as if he was drunk, and ran his fingers through his tangled, curly, black hair. For a moment, Pierce wondered if it was Kalen Rusk, but a second look at the man told him otherwise.

"Hey, I, uh...was just passin' through the neighborhood," he said, forcing himself to properly pronounce each word.

"And?" Lisabeth replied.

"And...and...I was wondering if you had...wait. I got the wrong house. Oh, man. Sorry."

The man stumbled off of the front doorstep and wandered back toward the street. Lisabeth closed the front door and put her back against it.

Pierce came out from behind the kitchen wall with Suzanne in tow. "That was weird."

"I don't think he got the wrong house," Lisabeth said. "He looked like he wanted to come inside and look around. He kept trying to look around me."

"We should get out of here," he said to Suzanne. "Go wake James up."

Suzanne nodded and left for the guest bedroom.

Pierce returned to the kitchen and stood near their backpacks. As he surveyed his crossbow with a handful of arrows in a makeshift quiver, he felt angry with himself for not putting up a public fight against Kalen. Although he was not versed in the realm of sabotage, he knew enough about the infrastructure of the city to cause great disruption. In the end, what would he gain? Would it just feed into

Kalen's public portrayal of him anyway?

When Suzanne returned to the living room, she led James over to the sofa. Pierce stood next to her. She whispered into Pierce's ear. "We should pray first."

Pierce let of a sigh of anguish. "Pray about what?"

"Just trust me."

She clasped his hands and he held on tight to hers. She closed her eyes and bowed her head. "Lord, please help us to make the right decision."

Although Pierce heard her words, he focused on other things in the room instead.

After a moment, Suzanne stared into his eyes. "God said to wait."

"Wait? Wait for what? Our friends have been taken away. People are getting thrown into arenas to get killed and it's time to wait?"

"I don't know. That was the word that came to me before I even finished speaking."

He took another deep breath and headed back to the kitchen. "So why isn't God talking to me? You said he was going to raise up people. Where are they? You said they would be all around us. Looks to me like they're getting dragged off against their will."

He slung his backpack over his shoulder and then picked up the quiver. He scooped up the crossbow and clenched it with an angry fist. "Let's go."

James gathered up his backpack of belongings. His hands trembled.

There was a somber, almost palpable sense of foreboding in the kitchen now and Pierce knew it. He was not sure where it was coming from or if they were headed on the right course, but he knew that sometimes he was supposed to act. He knew God would come to their aid in a time of need. Or at least that's what he thought he read the last time he looked in the Bible.

As they headed out the back door, Lisabeth tapped Suzanne's shoulder. They embraced for a moment and then she said, "Let me know where you are going. Please keep in touch. Stay safe." Tears began to trickle down her cheek as Suzanne tore herself away from the moment.

The three of them headed out onto Mandelbrot Curve and toward the trap door entrance a block away from City Hall. Pierce continually scanned the streets around them, peered in between houses, and watched the skies for busybees. So far tonight the streets were empty, no one lurked between the houses, and air was free of electric eyes.

* * *

As they passed near downtown, Pierce caught sight of the giant hourglass erected in Meres Park in honor of this endeavor. The hourglass stood some fifty feet tall, with a rounded, polished, aluminum base and top. The top of the hourglass was filled with blood-red sand that trickled into a mounting pile far beneath. He felt his fist tighten around his crossbow. One well placed strike with an arrow just might shatter the glass.

"If we had time, I'd take that thing right out," he muttered to Suzanne.

As he stared at the red grains tumbling through the hourglass, it made him think it was as if the heart and soul of the city itself were being drained out from underneath it. Everything was crumbling before their eyes and to think he helped to build the robotic army that held them hostage made him shudder. He had heard rumors that the busybees had spread throughout all of the settlements, and economic pressure was being applied to all of them to give up the remaining believers.

Up ahead in the distance, he saw a wisp of black smoke rising from a nearby warehouse. Soon the wisp became a plume and shouts could be heard from down the street. The threat of fire and disease were the two prime things that kept the mayors of the settlements up at night. Both could spread with lightning rapidity, but fire, if it got out of control, could take lives, property, and the air they breathed. There were no solid contingency plans in place should a fire escalate to the point of taking out several buildings and overwhelming the pressurization systems of the city. The only plan that Pierce knew of was to run to escape asphyxiation.

Within minutes, several Cyclode Sentinels arrived and hooked up hoses to the city's water system. Smoke still billowed into the domed sky but at a slower pace until it stopped altogether. The stench of burned plastic hung in the air as they scrambled toward the trap door in the street.

Before they could turn the final corner, an ion coil shot pummeled the street in front of them. It left a perfect dimple in the surface of the street and sent up its own tiny plume of smoke.

Pierce looked up to see a third-generation Cyclode fifty feet ahead of them, with an ion coil weapon aimed at his head. He stopped running and lifted up his crossbow high in the air. His backpack of belongings hit the street with a defeated thud. James clutched Suzanne's hand as they stood next to Pierce.

"Now what?" Suzanne whispered with trembling in her voice.

"If we split up we may have a chance. But we should all try to reconvene at the trap door."

Just as the three of them began to separate, another Cyclode marched out from behind a nearby house. Pierce changed his mind and told them, "Run, but in a zigzag pattern. They can't handle that."

The three of them separated and ran away from each other. In one swift motion, Pierce grabbed an arrow out of his quiver and lowered his hands only to fire a shot at the Cyclode's head. He reloaded the bow and fired another shot at the machine's ion coil weapon which knocked its firing trajectory off course. He ran back to pick up his belongings and bolted off again.

More shots were fired at them and he speculated they were meant to stun and not kill. He dove in between a pair of houses and prepared his bow again. Suzanne screamed.

He looked back and saw a man standing next to her. The man, whom he recognized as the mechanic he met back in the Chinese Restaurant while he was still mayor, fired his own ion coil pistol at the two Cyclodes that closed in on them. Each shot seemed only to stall and not disable the marching menaces. Pierce knew the machines were hardened against such shots, until one of them suddenly dropped to its mechanical knees.

Suzanne ran toward Pierce. He launched another arrow at the lead Cyclode but it flew wide and to the left. He clutched her hand and together they ran toward James. In the confusion and the ensuing gunfire, the mechanic continued to pour shots into each machine and knocked them off course just enough. The three of them raced toward the trap door in the street and when they reached it, Pierce wrenched it open.

As he hurried them inside, he looked back one last time upon the city. On a furniture store down the street, neon orange nanoparticle graffiti appeared, changed, then disappeared every other minute. One message read: "Long Live Io" and another read "See you at Camp Io". None of it made sense to him, unless it was Kyrk running through the streets again. The graffiti even shifted to cover a Dove League poster before moving on.

He fired off the last of his arrows and it punctured the ankle joint of another Cyclode. Out of arrows, he threw the crossbow aside.

Together they climbed down the stairwell and under the city. After all of them were inside the tunnel, Pierce shut the latch behind them and turned on his flashlight. He swung the light around to make sure they were all safe. They traveled several yards and came to a junction in the system.

"I didn't expect him to help out. Of all people," he said.

"Know what he told me?" Suzanne said. "He said he didn't agree with some of your policies as mayor, but you were better than the clown we got in there now."

Pierce smirked. Maybe he did have some allies in the city after all. "Did you notice his badge color? Bright orange. Considering the way he was firing at the Cyclodes, don't you find it odd he wasn't picked up by the Network as a threat?"

"Bad algorithms," James said.

"Maybe there's some hope after all. Question is, how do we exploit that?"

"He did say he wanted us to say hi to Omar," Suzanne added.

Pierce thought about this a moment. Perhaps the mechanic had worked on Omar's vehicle at some point in the past. Maybe the mechanic even knew a few people who had direct contact with the Network servers and somebody conveniently altered his profile. Or, the mechanic's own research changed his badge color.

He set his backpack down and noticed the zipper had come undone. He peered inside and scoped around to make sure all his belongings were intact.

"Uh oh," he said as he rustled around inside his backpack.

"What?" James replied.

"I dropped my notebook somewhere."

"Your notebook?"

"My notebook." He looked up to shine the flashlight into the boy's face. "I had a notebook of plans. City plans. Great plans, really."

He swept the flashlight back down the corridor but did not see any signs of his notebook. Up above, he heard more gunfire. Then an explosion shook the walls of the tunnel. Dust sifted down on top of them.

"Okay, let's keep moving." Pierce zipped up his backpack and led the three of them toward the next tunnel junction. The air quality was not the best under here but at least the smoke smell had not reached them.

As they crept ahead, he recalled seeing a video years ago about the opening day festivities of Magnopolis, and how Jack Addard spoke of a newfound heartbeat of the city. The video referenced a marching band in the background and a player pounding on a bass drum. Now the bass drum had been replaced by gunfire and like the hourglass on the street above, the very life of the city was now in danger of being drained away for good.

Chapter Nineteen

As they scampered through the tunnel system, the explosions continued above them. Gunfire echoed throughout the corridors as if an all-out battle erupted just after they left. As they came upon junction after junction, Pierce realized the tunnel system was far more extensive than he imagined. "Why didn't anybody ever tell me about this?" He wondered aloud.

Pierce sensed they had to be coming up to the edge of the city. A sign up ahead pointed toward another hallway and simply said, "Garage".

When they reached the entrance to the garage, he gave the door handle a gentle tug. It did not give way at first and only after several more pulls did it pop open. They soon found another set of stairs leading up to another door. Suzanne led the way up the stairs. The next door opened up into a maintenance garage.

Inside the garage several six-wheeled sand crawlers sat in a row, although he did not recognize any of them. Next to the crawlers were three monowheel machines, each with two seats apiece. Each monowheel stood eight feet tall and was equipped with two side guns. The main wheel was made up of two thick spiked tires set just apart from each other for rolling over the desert sand.

"So much for my map drawing skills," Pierce said.

"Did we bring our keys?" Suzanne said, trying to make light of the situation.

"This isn't our garage. I think it's the west garage."

"But we don't have any pressure suits," James said with a shaking sound in his voice.

"Not to worry. There are always plenty of those in a garage. There's some over there against the wall. Hopefully we can find one your size." Pierce jogged over to the wall and scrounged around for a suitable suit. After minutes of searching, he found one and held it out to James.

"How long do you think it will be before they find us?" Suzanne said as she slipped into a pressure suit of her own.

"I figure we have about a half hour. Those machines can't get into the tunnels anyway. The busybees can, but I didn't see them follow us inside."

"I thought you said you spotted sensors everywhere."

"I did. But that was on the streets and on the streetlights. I doubt there were any sensors in the tunnels. By the way, what color do you think my badge is now?"

"I haven't checked. Isn't it orange?"

"I'd guess brown."

"Where is your badge anyway?"

"I flushed it down the toilet before we left."

As soon as all three of them donned their suits, James walked over to one of the monowheel machines. He climbed inside and studied the controls.

"Sorry, bud. We can't use those. No keys," Pierce said.

James glanced back at Pierce but then turned back to face the machine's console. He studied the machine and then popped the side cover off of the steering wheel. After a few seconds of study, he pulled out some wires and reattached them.

The moment he plugged one of the wires back in, the monowheel engine started up with a roar. The machine settled down to a low idle, but still sounded like a muffled jet airplane engine. James turned back toward his Mom and smiled wide.

James jumped down off the machine and climbed into the next one. A minute later, he fired up that machine and waved toward Pierce.

"Maybe I don't want to know where he learned that skill," Pierce said.

Suzanne climbed into the second machine but James jumped down. He ran over toward Pierce who climbed into the first monowheel.

Pierce looked back to see James fastening his shoulder harness. He then looked over at Suzanne, who gave him a big smile.

"Let's roll," she said with a grin.

Pierce fastened his own shoulder harness and pressed the garage door opener button on the console. The inner airlock door opened before them at too slow of a pace for his comfort. When the first door lifted, they rolled their machines inside. He hit the opener button again.

The outer airlock door crawled open to reveal a dark, cold, and desolate landscape covered in baseball-sized stones. The sky was stunningly clear, unlike anything he had ever seen on Earth, and the stars shone with piercing brilliance.

The inside of their monowheel was a study in high-end electronics, with gyroscopes and gears visible all around them. The console in front of Pierce appeared simple but it took him a few minutes to adjust to curves and rolling over bumps. Despite the bubble-shaped cockpit, he knew they were less safe than inside of a sand crawler in case of an accident.

He flipped on the console radio and attempted to hail the other machine. "Suzanne. Can you hear me?"

Suzanne rolled along behind him in her machine. She radioed back. "I can hear you. What's your plan?"

"The plan is to get to the Freeland settlement. They seem to be the least likely to go along with all of this."

"Lead the way then."

Pierce nodded and turned the grip on the accelerator. He brought up a glowing navigation map from the console and punched in new coordinates. The terrain in this part of the desert was flat but Pierce noticed the size of the boulders continued to increase. Although the shock system of the monowheel buffered them from many of the bumps, the first priority would be to find the flattest, most obstacle-free path.

As the Magnopolis dome faded behind them on the horizon, Pierce felt a sense of isolation under a dazzling canopy of stars. Phobos was about a quarter of the way up in the sky and he knew that daylight would come over the horizon in the next few hours. The dual headlights from his machine cast an eerie reddish glow in front of them and the light cast from Suzanne's machine projected shadows inside his cockpit.

He steered his vehicle up onto the trans-desert highway that ran to the Freeland settlement and Suzanne followed. A handful of bright green specks soon appeared on the forward radar.

"Suzanne. Are you looking at the radar?" Pierce said.

"I sure am. What do you think they are?"

"I don't know but I count five of them. In formation. And they are all heading this way down the highway. I think we need to go off-roading again."

"Agreed. Lead the way."

Pierce steered their monowheel back off of the road but the formation mirrored their moves and began to close in. "Looks like they have a bead on us. I don't have a visual yet. The night vision scope isn't showing anything yet either."

"Think they're Cyclodes?"

"Could be. At least this time we have guns."

"You really think we should take them on?"

"I thought you wanted to fight?"

"I do. I just meant…if we don't have to, why risk it?"

Pierce turned slightly to look back at James. "How good are you at firing ion weapons?"

James looked to his side. He fingered the firing control handle and buttons for the weapons. "I learn fast."

In minutes the threat became visual. On the edge of the horizon, several third-generation Cyclode Sentinels marched toward them. Pierce first saw the tops of their helmets, and then their shoulders, with their weapons drawn. "Get ready," he radioed to Suzanne.

Before he gave the signal to James, the Cyclodes opened fire. Wave after wave of ion coil fire was directed into their path, but it was unclear whether they were trying to destroy the monowheels or merely cripple them. James opened fire. Suzanne rolled up alongside them and targeted the lead machines.

Clouds of dust sprang up before them like rusted iron fountains that moved in slow motion. Pierce cheered as one of the Cyclodes dropped to its mechanical knees while another toppled over into the sand. "Good shot, kid," he said to James.

The next wave of fire fanned out in an arc and nicked his machine and hit Suzanne's monowheel near the engine. Her machine wobbled a bit, then threw her into a nauseating spin that tossed her and the cockpit around and around like a gerbil. James intensified his return fire and took out the machine that hit their monowheels.

Pierce slowed his machine to a halt and pivoted around to come to Suzanne's rescue. As he accelerated toward her the crossfire intensified to the point where he knew he could be putting their machine in grave danger. James spun around in his seat and the weapons rotated with him. Again he opened fire on their pursuers.

Pierce felt like he was reliving a painful piece of personal history in seeing her machine disabled. Instead of watching it on video from his living room telescreen, he now had a front row seat in real time. It was then that he saw another pair of Cyclodes and a transport rolling right up behind her machine.

"Suzanne!" He shouted through the radio, but of course it was no good.

Repeatedly, he was driven back by the intense crossfire around them. The transport stopped, and under protection of ion coil fire, two men in brick-red pressure suits ran over to her disabled machine. Before he could wheel the machine into position so that James could open fire on the transport, she was gone.

Chapter Twenty

Pierce slammed his fist against the steering wheel in anger. If not for James in the back seat, he would have plunged straight at the Cyclode formation around the transport and hammered at the machines until his own machine was taken out. Now he had to think about whether to pursue or continue on their treacherous course to the Freeland settlement. He looked back at James. There was a look of fear in the boy's eyes that Pierce had not seen before.

Pierce glanced back at the radar and formulated an escape route on the fly. "I have an idea. I think we can head back toward the Freeland settlement. But there are some hills and rock formations we can hide behind if needed. After we lose these guys, then we can circle back and look for your Mom. I know where they're taking her."

"You do?"

"Unfortunately. History's repeating itself only this time it's on a bigger scale. But like before, we'll figure this out."

James only nodded.

As Pierce looked over the radar map, he triangulated the distance between their current location, the Freeland settlement, and the Chronopticus Complex. Somewhere near the Chronopticus Complex was the wreckage of Io. He thought about the nanoparticle graffiti he saw back in Magnopolis. *Was someone building a rebel base near where Io fell into the dust? Or were they planning on resurrecting the machine? Were any of the Cyclodes under rebel control? Is there a chance Suzanne was taken to a rebel base?*

None of the theoretical answers to those questions reassured him. As he realigned his course to parallel that of the highway running between the settlements, more Cyclodes appeared on the highway and started to head toward them. He took a deep breath and shook his head.

Before he could gun the engine, the monowheel shuddered as if it had been hit. The odor of smoke soon began to fill the cockpit and the radar went black. Another shot glanced off of the front of the monowheel and hit their engine.

"Dad!" James shouted.

A second later they were sent into a tumbling gyration that bounced them off of a nearby boulder and knocked Pierce out cold.

* * *

When Pierce awoke, he found himself flat on his back and on an uncomfortable bed. His pressure suit and helmet were gone, which caused him to panic for a moment. Then, as he regained his bearings and surveyed his surroundings, he realized what had happened.

He was now inside the Chronopticus prison complex.

He sat up and instinctively called out to James. There was no reply.

He called out again, but this time he heard Suzanne's voice from behind the cell wall to the left of him.

"He's not here, Pierce," she said.

"Where are you?"

"In the cell next to you."

He stood up, but struggled as his legs gave out beneath him. He reached out and clutched the bars on the front of his cell before regaining his footing. "Are you okay? Have you seen James?"

"I'm okay. A little dazed, but okay. I didn't see James anywhere. What happened to you out there?"

"Last thing I remember I was plotting out a new course to try and shake the Cyclodes off us. Then we were going to circle back and pick you up. But I think we got hit. It's kind of blur. Did you get a look at the people that brought you in?"

"No. I did see the two that brought you in. You were out cold. They were a couple of big guys. Probably over six feet tall. I tried talking to them but they didn't respond."

Pierce wandered back over to his bed and sat down. His legs were still like rubber. He ran his fingers through his hair and found new lumps forming but no blood. In the fog of his recovery, thoughts of lost freedom, James, his missing notebook, and the fate of the city swirled around in his mind like a toxic brew.

In despair, he looked around at his cell, the dirt on the floor, and then at his outfit. He groaned as he spotted a new food badge attached to his shirt. It was bright red in color as if he crossed some algorithmic point of no return. Then he remembered he stowed something in one of the pants pockets. He withdrew a small Bible that fit in the palm of his hand and set it on the bed next to him.

"Pierce? You there?" Suzanne said.

"I'm here. Sorry. I just remembered something."

"What?"

He lowered his voice and glanced around to see if anyone was pacing the floor in the hallway between the cells. "I snuck in a book."

"A book? I was hoping you brought something else in that could get us out of here." Her voice was laden with sarcasm.

"I did what you did. I brought in a Bible."

Although he could not see her face, he knew she was smiling.

"Maybe you can teach us both something new," she said after a pause.

"You know when we were running out of the city, I couldn't help but look back at that stupid hourglass in downtown."

"And?"

"And it was like hope was being drained out of the city. Maybe even faith. Think Kalen has any faith?"

"Ha!" She said with a laugh. "In what? Himself?"

Pierce smiled and opened up his miniature Bible. The font was ridiculously small, but still legible. "Know what else happened out there?"

"Tell me."

"James called me Dad. He's never done that before. After you told me about the loss of his Dad I always hesitated when the subject came up."

"Why?"

"Because I called him son once and he didn't like it."

Suzanne sighed. "Remember what I said about walls? He's put up a few of his own, too. He just doesn't want to get hurt again."

Pierce sat in silence for a minute.

She continued. "James needs you. And by the way, I think you'd made a wonderful father. You're the best Dad I could imagine for him."

Pierce smiled again and said quietly, "Thanks."

He lay back on his bed and turned some pages. He reflected on how Kalen had killed the pastor, the watchmaker, and now was probably going to try and kill them. His mind remained ill at ease because he knew they had little to no control over the situation and little hope of escape. His eyes fell upon the opening verses of Psalm 121. They read, "I will lift up mine eyes unto the hills, from whence cometh my help. My help cometh from the Lord, which made heaven and earth."

Chapter Twenty-One

Pierce was jolted awake by a rumbling noise. As he opened his eyes dust sifted down on top of him. Concerned it was another tremor he sat up and then paced the floor of his cell like a caged lion. Breakfast was served to him on an aluminum tray that reminded him of a television dinner he once ate back on Earth. Breakfast consisted of reconstituted, powdered, scrambled eggs, a paper-thin slice of ham, and hash browns. Neither the eggs nor the ham resembled what he remembered from Earth. The hash browns tasted authentic yet the plastic cup of sealed orange juice made him wonder if any of this food or drink was drugged.

Since there were no windows inside the prison, he wondered how long he was going to last without actual sunlight filtering through. The artificial lights embedded into the ceiling and the walls threw multiple odd-colored shadows off of everything they touched. All of this made him pine for a settled life back on Earth, maybe even running his own architectural firm.

He pushed aside his breakfast tray. He longed to spend a week at his parents' old log cabin on Lake Vermillion, looking out upon the water from a boat as he dropped his fishing line into the depths for an afternoon of walleye fishing. He then reminisced of the times when a lightning storm would drive him off the lake. Watching the clouds roil on high as the waves smashed the shoreline could only be countered by a hot cup of cocoa and a good book. Of course there were no natural rivers or lakes here on Mars and the farm-raised fish they sold at the market never tasted right anyway.

He flipped open his Bible and picked up where he left off last night. By now he was in chapter twelve of the book of Romans, and the opening verses spoke of presenting one's body as a living sacrifice to God. It then spoke of not being conformed to the world and being transformed by the renewing of the mind.

He looked up. "Suzanne, you up?"

A half-minute passed without a word from her. Then: "Barely. I didn't sleep all that well last night."

"Did you ever read Romans?"

She shifted on her bed. "I think so. Why?"

"There's a part about being a living sacrifice. Do you think they are going to send us to the lion pit like they did with the others?"

"I hope not," Suzanne said as her breakfast tray made a scraping sound against the dirt floor.

"Maybe I should do a study on lions," Pierce muttered.

"Of course they'll send us out there," a man said from across the hallway.

Pierce looked over at the cell across from him. The man looked to be in his thirties, with thinning hair, a gaunt face, and eyes that were sunken slightly. "You really think they plan on that?"

The man's face became sour. "A lot of people have been run through there. Some make it out, some don't."

Pierce sat up straight. "Were you here when Lynn got injured?"

"Lynn? Not sure who you mean."

Pierce described her looks and then Omar's appearance.

"Oh, right. Yeah, I was here. Been here a while. Lost track of the days. Yeah, she was the strangest one. Thought for sure she was a goner but she got up."

"I think she was healed," Suzanne said out of nowhere.

The man nodded. "Was that what it was? She's in the other cell block, but yeah, I remember that." Then the man pointed toward the book in Pierce's hand. "Have one of those to spare?"

Pierce shook his head no. "No, but I'll share mine in a little while if you want."

"Read those verses out loud. I want to hear them," the man said.

Pierce focused again on the page. "I beseech you therefore, brethren, by the mercies of God, that ye present your bodies a living sacrifice, holy, acceptable unto God, which is your reasonable service. And be not conformed to this world: but be ye transformed by the renewing of your mind, that ye may prove what is that good, and acceptable, and perfect, will of God." He looked up to gauge the man's reaction.

At this point, the man's eyes were closed, as if to tune out anything else that might distract him. "Thanks," he said after a moment. "It's talking about God. And your mind. Not so much about lions."

Pierce nodded. "Right." He glanced over at the man's badge and noticed it was a dark orange, although one could never be sure under these phony sunlamps. He looked down at his own badge and noticed no change in the color. He started in again, "For I say, through the grace given unto me, to every man that is among you, not to think of himself more highly than he ought to think; but to think soberly, according as God hath dealt to every man the measure of faith. For as we have many members in one body, and all members have not the same office."

He paused and looked down again at his badge and then at the man across the hallway. "Notice something?"

"What?"

"Our badges. They're not changing anymore."

The two men exchanged glances.

"Maybe they forgot to install sensors here. Or microphones," Suzanne said as she pushed her tray back across the floor.

"Maybe we've found a hole in the algorithms," Pierce said. "It's not like their reading our minds. At least not yet." He looked back down at the book in his hands and it made him all the more eager to keep reading.

After a minute, he looked up again. He waved over to his companion across the hallway. "By the way, name's Pierce Steadman. Former mayor of Magnopolis."

The man smiled. "I'm Anyk. Still a carpenter. Nice to meet ya."

Anyk reached into his pants pocket and pulled out a set of cobalt blue dice. He set them into his right hand and extended his hand through the bars. There were seven dice in all. "Want to play a game of dice?"

Pierce moved toward the bars on the front of his cell. He leaned over to look. The dice did not look like a typical set of dice and appeared to be metallic cubes with rounded edges. They resembled the dice he saw in Artelius' shop on the day he bought the wedding ring for Suzanne. "Where'd you get those?"

"Some kid sold them to me on the street."

"Which kid?"

"Looked to be about ten or twelve. Dark brown hair. About this tall." Anyk extended a hand up a few feet from the floor. "Why? You know 'em?"

Pierce studied the dice again. "They look...familiar. Sue, don't those look like the machines James used to play with?"

For the first time this morning, Pierce could see his girlfriend's face through the other bars, if barely. Her long brown hair draped just through the bars until she swept it back with her hand. The scene bought a moment of levity to his morning.

"Was the kid named James?" She said.

"I don't know. You know 'em? These dice are way heavier than any I remember back on Earth. Maybe it's the gravity or something."

"The same dice on Earth would be lighter up here," she replied. "It looks like something my son was playing with. Those aren't ordinary dice."

The man shook the dice in his fist and threw them against his cell wall. They bounced off the wall and tumbled back to the floor. Besides that, they did nothing.

"Did he make 'em?" Anyk said.

"No."

"Well, they act like ordinary dice."

"Try dropping one chest-high, but with the number one turned up," Suzanne advised.

Anyk picked up a single die and turned it so that the number one faced up. He held it chest-high and dropped it to the floor. After a bounce the die sat motionless for several seconds.

Suddenly, the die started to turn by itself on the floor. Four tiny metal blades sprang out of its sides and then pointed down toward the floor. As the die spun, it began to pile up a ring of dirt around it.

Anyk scuttled back a few feet. "It's digging. Digging into the floor."

"Tap it. On top. With another die," Suzanne said.

Anyk picked up another die and hit the first one on top. The die stopped spinning and withdrew its blades. He picked it up and held it out for the others to see. "What is this thing?"

"They're tunnelers. Someone must have another MatterForge up here. How many of those do you have?"

"Maybe a dozen."

"Try one more thing for me. Take that die again and make a circle on the floor. Make it a few feet across. Then pick it up and drop it in the middle of the circle with the number one turned up again."

Anyk followed Suzanne's instructions and dropped the die. Again, it began to spin, but this time it carved out an arc until it reached the edge of the drawn circle. Then, it followed the track carved in the dirt and began to dig with its blades spinning.

Pierce smiled and so did Anyk. "I'll share my book if you share some of those dice."

"Deal," Anyk said without hesitation. He rolled a blue die across the floor toward Pierce and tossed another one toward Suzanne's cell. He then pitched more of the dice toward Suzanne and Pierce and motioned on either side of their cells.

Pierce took one die for himself and rolled several more to his left. From the neighboring cell, a hand reached out, pulled one die in, and passed the rest down the line.

Anyk looked over toward Suzanne. "I think I know what they did with your son."

Pierce's eyes widened.

"I think they probably sent him back home. That's what they did with mine. Do you have any other relatives on the outside?"

"My sister. She wasn't taken in," Suzanne said.

"He's probably safe then."

Pierce picked up his die and drew a circle in the dirt that was three feet across. He then dropped the die in the middle and waited. The die spun around, stuck out its blades, and began to whirl its way toward the edge of the circle. In no time it worked its way around the circle and left a tiny ring of powder in its wake.

"Are they going to keep us in here all day?" Pierce wondered aloud as he watched the die circle about on the floor.

"No, they'll let us out for lunch. Dinner, too," a voice said from down the hallway.

* * *

When lunchtime came, Pierce, Suzanne, Anyk, and the others were guided by the Cyclodes into the cafeteria complex Pierce had only glimpsed at before. There, he saw several dozen people, including Omar, Lynn, Ruelle, and Ryan. Omar looked weary as if he lost several pounds of weight and struggled to keep his shoulders upright.

Pierce held Suzanne's hand as they moved toward the serving line. He could not help but notice the abundance of telescreens on the walls, all tuned to the same monotonous news channel. He read the news scroll across the bottom of one screen, which mentioned the recent quakes. A map had been made of the tremors and all of the epicenters were in the area of the mountain that housed the Chronopticus Network complex and prison facilities. Perhaps more tunneling work was underway nearby or maybe the mountain they were in was awakening to life.

The news then cut away to a scene of a Magnopolis city street. In the center of the video, a man dressed in jeans and a black hooded sweatshirt stood under a city street light during the night. The video showed the man looking up and saying something as if he were having a conversation with the light. The angle was poor and image of the man's face was fuzzy.

The anchor then reappeared and went on to explain how some wondered if he was responsible for the recent rash of nanoparticle graffiti across the city. Messages such as "Long Live Io" and "See you at Io" appeared on building walls and then disappeared when the police arrived. No one knew exactly what the slogans meant, but the anchor speculated it referred to some secret rebel base that the Dexler corporate government would soon deal with.

Pierce knew better, though. He turned and leaned over to whisper into Suzanne's ear. "If we get out of here, and I ever go back to being a mayor, remind me to find a way to get Kyrk to work with me. He got more guts than I've seen in a long time."

"I wonder why they let him go on like that?"

"Maybe they think he's delusional. I happen to think he's on to something."

They moved forward in the serving line and reached the area where food was being dispensed by a series of automated food service robots. An aluminum tray dropped down onto the metal conveyor belt before Suzanne. The robot then dispensed a blob of pseudo-mashed potatoes, a chunk of gray meatloaf, and a scoop of abnormally bright green peas. Pierce received the same meal and the trays continued on down the line making a clacking sound against the segmented conveyor belt.

The next food service robot reached out with a metal chute and dumped a few wedges of purple-skinned pepperfruit onto Suzanne's tray. The machine then dumped a portion onto his tray.

"So this is Eden, huh?" Pierce said. "Fruit from a talking tree."

Chapter Twenty-Two

The next time breakfast rolled around, it was yet another variation on the same tasteless theme. Today there were dehydrated, reconstituted, reassembled gray sausage links on Pierce's plate along with pancakes that had a sandpaper texture in his mouth but no flavor. He spit out the latter and realized he was on the fast track to a weight loss plan. Yet as soon as he had pushed the tray aside and spent a few minutes in his Bible, the familiar crunch-crunch sound of metallic legs on rock filled the nearby hallway.

He looked up to see a Cyclode Sentinel followed by a pair of human guards dressed in slate-blue uniforms with Dexler logos on their chests. He turned back to his reading, hoping to ignore their presence, but was startled a moment later when one of the guards rapped on the bars of his cell with a black baton.

"Get up, Steadman. It's time for the games," the guard barked.

"What games? I'm not really in the mood for any games. Except maybe dice." Pierce glanced down at the floor and at the faint ring of dirt in front of his bed. As far as he knew the tunneler had been grinding through the floor throughout the night and would probably hit the next level below within days.

"Kalen never said you were a smart-aleck. Time to go, Steadman," the guard said. The man opened Pierce's cell door by passing his hand over the lock.

Pierce stuffed his book under his pillow and stood up. He paced over to the door but took as long as he could. Suzanne was already out in the hallway and he gave her a wink. Meanwhile, Anyk snored away in bed.

The other guard raked his baton across the bars on Anyk's cell and startled the man out of bed. Pierce rolled his eyes and then coughed as the baton was driven into his back. Along with several other inmates they were marched down the corridor to waiting surface transports inside the garage of the prison complex. The dark rock hallways were dimly lit and it was not a passageway Pierce had seen before. He tried to remember as much as he could since this path would make an ideal escape route. Once they were loaded into the transports, the prisoners were shuttled across the desert toward Magnopolis.

The prisoners in Pierce's transport remained silent for most of the trip until he spoke up. "So have you figured it out yet?" He said to one of the guards.

"Figured what out?" The guard replied, uninterested. He did not look at Pierce.

"Eden."

"What are you talking about?"

"Have you figured out how to build your own Eden yet? I read all about the Eden Project. You're probably too young to remember Gordyn Karst. He saw all this coming years ahead of time."

The guard did not reply.

"But see, if I get killed today, everything will be alright. I'll still survive, but in a different place."

Suzanne glared at him, but he pressed on.

"See, you can bump us off and God will just keep sending you more of us. What's more is your algos can't see in here or in here." Pierce pointed first to his heart and then to his forehead. "Besides, this place isn't yours anyway. It never was."

The guard chuckled and turned away.

At that, the transport slowed its forward roll and came to a stop. A few seconds later, it rolled forward again until it came to another stop. The air brakes hissed like startled snakes and voices could be heard coming from outside the vehicle. Two raps were given on the door from the outside and both guards stood at attention, each armed with an ion coil rifle. They both looked around at the group and the guard Pierce argued with earlier seemed ready to push Pierce out the door first.

Soon the elliptical door on the side of the transport opened and all the prisoners were escorted out. Pierce found himself inside of a large holding airlock, which he recognized as being one of the entrances to Magnopolis. They then passed through another airlock and back into the city.

He could smell a tinge of smoke in the air, as if another building had burned since the night he and Suzanne fled town. He did not see any stray graffiti on any of the buildings they passed, although he did see a homeowner tending to a broken living room picture window.

In minutes they arrived at one of the side entry gates to the Coliseum. They were then led into a tunnel which ran underneath the building. At the end of the tunnel, a steel gate slid sideways to admit them. Beyond the gate they were corralled into a holding area with a dozen lockers on either side of a set of benches. Between the benches was a pile of swords and metal armor on the floor. Pierce recognized the armor as the same cheap protection that was given to Omar and his wife during the battle he watched from the stands.

"You know what to do," one of the guards said in a gruff voice.

Pierce, along with the others, walked toward the pile and began to sort through the armor. The swords were all the same length, less than a yard long apiece, and the armor only protected one's upper body. Buried in the pile were a handful of shields. He lifted up one of the shields and realized why no one else used them. Each shield was so heavy that he was sure it was meant to slow a person down rather than help them.

"Look at them," the guard said to another. "Like rats diggin' through the trash."

Just as Suzanne reached down to grab one of the swords, the guard stepped over and kicked it across the floor and out of her reach. He followed his gesture with a grating laugh.

Pierce, who stood next to Suzanne, turned and charged the guard with all his strength. He knocked the brute back several feet. "What's your problem?" He said as he pushed both of his hands against the guard's chest.

Out of the corner of his eye, Pierce could see one of the Cyclode Sentinels that stood along the wall raise its ion coil pistol at him. He reached again for the guard but the guard shoved him back.

"Easy, now, big shot," the guard laughed, unconcerned at what just happened. "And when you folks are done here you can follow me into the holding room."

Pierce wondered if anyone in their group realized that they were all armed now and could very well mutiny and battle their way out of here. As he glanced around the room, he analyzed the group's collective physical abilities and thought better of it.

* * *

By the time they dressed, they were led into another nearby holding chamber. The door at the far end of the chamber was made of grated steel, and through it Pierce could see a metal elevator platform that led to the surface. Light poured into the elevator shaft as a trap door on the floor of the arena opened up. He could hear the cheers and jeers of the crowd as they responded to the announcer over the Coliseum loudspeaker. He reached over and held Suzanne's hand and stared into her eyes. "Whatever happens," he said, feeling his chest tighten up, "I've got your back."

Suzanne began to shake and sob. Then she closed her eyes. "I can't do this."

"Look at me," he said as he set down his sword and put both hands on her shoulders.

"I can't. I...I want to go home. I want to go home now."

There was a frightened distance in her eyes as her cheeks became pale. He could see sweat beading up on her forehead and it reminded him of the syndrome that would sometimes hit new settlers that just arrived from Earth. Some, within days of their arrival on Mars, would fall into a near-neurotic state called "Homesteader's Panic". It would always start with a simple reminiscing of being back on Earth and then spiral into a realization that many of the items people took for granted back home were non-existent up here. Then came thoughts of losing contact with family members and friends. Soon the physical symptoms would set in and sometimes it sent people to the psychiatric ward in the medical hub. In the end, about half of those affected boarded the next rocket back home.

"Stay with me," Pierce said. "We are going to go home. We're going to get through this." He pulled her tight into his arms but it did little to relieve her trembling. "James needs you. I need you."

He pulled back and she nodded her head in affirmation. She wiped her eyes and nose on the sleeve of her shirt and picked up her sword again.

"Let's knock these beasts into orbit, okay?" He said, trying to fire up what little reserves of energy she probably had left. He picked up his own sword again and held her hand. Inside, he felt his heart trying to tear its way out of his ribcage like a jailed animal.

As the gate lifted into the ceiling, the guards shoved the group forward. There were six prisoners in all, including Pierce, Suzanne, and four others. The six of them stepped forward on to the elevator platform. Pierce stared up and saw the roof of the Magnopolis dome since there was no roof on the Coliseum. Upstairs there was cheering, while down here they were readying themselves to die. The elevator platform jerked to life and lifted them to the surface, as the announcer's voice became clearer.

"And to our contestants, may the algorithms watch over you!" The announcer said as they reached the level of the playing field.

"Where's Midori when you need her?" Pierce said quietly. He held up his sword. "Anybody here trained in how to use these things?"

The group did not reply.

They stepped out onto the playing field, tentative at first, and then in wary awe as the crowds stared down at them from above. Pierce reasoned the place was half full at best. Although the group stayed together in a tight cluster, Pierce eventually broke away and turned around to face the others.

He knelt down onto the playing field, which was made of some type of coarse mahogany-colored sand. Near his feet he could see drops of dried blood. All around them on the surface a grid of sharp, blue, laser-drawn hexagons appeared. He began to draw a diagram in the dirt with the tip of his sword.

"I have an idea. I took a good look at how the lions moved the last time we were here."

"The lions?" A man asked as he crouched down next to Pierce. The man was in his fifties, with a tall and lanky frame. He had wavy red hair with blue-green eyes and an Irish accent.

"They have mechanical lions. They're being housed over there," Pierce said, pointing toward another gated entrance to the arena area. "That's what the swords are for. The armor's no good, though. But here's what I'm thinking..."

He drew a circle in the dirt, and then six points inside the circle that represented the group. He then drew four marks to represent the lions as they approached the circle. "These lions all run off of algorithms and are controlled from somewhere in the stands. I don't know if there's a manual override for them, but they tend to move in predictable patterns."

The man who crouched down next to Pierce spoke up. "Do they have a full range of motion?"

"I think so. Now, their weak spot is at the base of the neck on the backside. They also like to gang up on individuals. But they seem to get confused when people run in zigzag motions."

"How do they handle collisions?" The man asked.

"I'm not sure what you mean."

"Has anybody ever gotten them to run into each other?"

Pierce gave him a puzzled look.

"Here." The man reached over and drew out a different design next to Pierce's drawing in the sand. "You say they don't like zigzag patterns. What if we all start out near the perimeter of the arena, but move toward the middle like this..." The man spoke slowly, yet methodically, with many pauses.

The man drew a strange pattern in the dirt that resembled a squared-off letter Y. He then expanded on the pattern so that it looked like a series of interconnected, squared-off letters. "Now if we all run these patterns with the lions on our tail and accelerate toward the middle..." He continued to draw lines in the sand and drew a collision point in the middle of his diagram. "It might be enough to throw off their vision and they'll collide in the middle. Then, we take off their heads with our swords."

Pierce reflected on this a minute and looked up at Suzanne. "What do you think?"

Suzanne stood with her arms crossed and shivered. "Let's just get this over with."

"Hope we can all run," Pierce said under his breath.

At the edge of the arena, a bell rang out.

Pierce and the man stood up. Pierce looked the rest of the group in the eyes and motioned for them to spread out in a semicircle. He figured they could station themselves near each of the four release gates of the lions and draw them in from there. He looked back at the man. "I didn't catch your name."

"It's Neal. Neal Rexilon."

Pierce nodded but then drew back.

"Oh, I'm not like my father. The one who brought the MatterForges up here. I am a mathematician, though."

Pierce smiled and sensed there was a lot more going on in Neal's mind than he was letting on about. He could not quite put his finger on it, but if he survived, he would ask about it later.

As the prisoners moved into place, Pierce stayed next to Suzanne's side. The steel grated gate before them lifted up to reveal a pair of glowing golden eyes. As the mechanical lion moved out onto the playing field, they backed up with their swords drawn.

"How fast can you run?" Suzanne said to Pierce in a whisper.

"Fast enough. How about you?"

"I took place first in conference finals once. In the fifty-yard dash," she said with a smile.

As they crept backwards, the mechanical lion matched them step for step. It snarled with a sound that reminded him of someone throwing a fistful of rocks inside of an empty metal garbage can.

"Let's start the pattern," he said as they continued their mechanized dance with death. The machine began to close the gap between them. Pierce yelled out, "Run!"

Pierce and Suzanne ran full speed toward the middle of the playing field, taking care to mimic the twists and turns Neal suggested. The others joined in the sprint to the middle. Pierce cringed at the thought of *them* colliding in the middle instead of the lions.

As fast as Pierce ran, Suzanne ran faster. At one point she flung off her armor and threw her sword aside, much to Pierce's dismay. He hurdled over her armor and pressed on toward the middle.

The crowd above rose to their feet in a staggered wave. When the group came within a few feet of each other, they darted off in different directions at the last moment. The four lions that closed in on them slammed into one another with a violent metal crunch. Each machine toppled over into a writhing heap.

Pierce stopped and spun around and drove his sword into one of the lions. The machine convulsed and smoked before its golden eyes faded out. Suzanne ran back for her sword and then took a swing at another lion that was trying to right itself. Neal swept in and both of them gashed the sides of the lion and then hit at its head. It, too, spit out a puff of smoke before its eyes blacked out.

The other two lions crept back up onto their feet, but now, all six prisoners swooped in and clobbered them incessantly. In minutes both lions were knocked out never to stand upright again.

Pierce glanced up to see Kalen in his own private box in the stands, wearing his garish Roman outfit as if he had been transported back in time to Rome. From here, even he could see the anger in Kalen's eyes.

He reached over to shake Neal's hand. The others reached over too, and before he knew it someone was praying a prayer of thanks. After they broke apart, he looked first into Suzanne's eyes and then up at the domed sky of Magnopolis.

Chapter Twenty-Three

By the time Pierce ate lunch in the cafeteria, the mood of the other prisoners lifted substantially. More than once, he found himself shaking hands with complete strangers who congratulated him for making a stand in the middle of the arena. Word had spread throughout the prison that the lions were able to be manipulated, if not defeated outright. Kalen, he figured, had to be fuming by now and he knew that it would not be long before the lions were reprogrammed to counteract any new strategies on the part of the prison population.

He felt a tap on his shoulder and turned around. It was another male prisoner who extended a hand to shake.

"Congratulations on the battle."

"It wasn't my idea. I mean, I had an idea, but Neal over there is the one who really figured it out." Pierce pointed across the cafeteria to a red-headed man sitting at one of the tables with a couple of other people.

As he moved through the line and picked up his food, he grimaced at the menu again. Lunch consisted of composite potatoes, a reconstituted pork cutlet shaped like a soggy brick, green beans, and gravy that resembled motor oil. Once he moved out of the queue and into the seating area, he sat down next to Neal and Suzanne.

Once there was a break in the conversation, Pierce asked a question that had been on his mind ever since the arena battle. "So tell me again. What was that pattern all about?"

Neal finished off a bite of potatoes with a straight face. "It was part of a Hilbert curve."

Pierce did not follow but nodded his head anyway.

"Basically, it's a simple form of recursion. A repeated pattern. I did some reading on Entner collisions the other day and put it together with what you told me. It was kind of a lark, but it worked."

"For now," Pierce countered. "You'd think they would have

figured that out ahead of time."

"Oh, they have. Or at least they know that there is an ongoing issue. They've abandoned a lot of robot designs but somehow they keep coming back to the same tried and true system and hope that the issue won't crop up. They tried to bury it in the software and in the equations, but it keeps reappearing."

Pierce mulled this over a moment.

Neal took another bite of potatoes. "Kind of like sin, if you think about it. Unless you deal with it the right way, it keeps coming back. The pattern keeps repeating. Even intensifying if you give it time."

Pierce and Suzanne both stopped eating and set their forks down.

Neal continued. "I've often wondered. Do you think sin is a fractal?"

"A fractal?" Suzanne said.

"A fractal is a pattern that you can magnify or reduce in size and at any scale, it's the same pattern."

Pierce gave him a deer-in-the-headlights look. The others at the table stopped eating as well.

Neal carried on. "I just read it again the other day in James where it says if you break one part of the Law you've broken the entire thing. Then in another part he asks what's causing fights among the people in the church and tells them their arguments are because they have struggles inside themselves. Now, what is war but a fight between groups of people? But at the end of the day, it reduces back down to individual sin. In other words, it's all about rebellion against God. And only one thing can break that pattern."

By now, the next table over stopped eating and listened.

"Sorry," Neal said with a blush. "Didn't mean to get all theological on you."

"No, it's okay," Pierce said as he leaned back and crossed his arms. "I was thinking about something last night. First, Kalen took God off the Network. When that didn't work, he closed down the church. Then he threw Pastor Capshaw in prison and had him killed. It's like he did everything he could to take God out of the picture, but he still can't take God out of here." Pierce pointed to the side of his forehead.

Neal and the others at the table smiled.

"So how is it you knew we'd make it out alive yesterday?"

Suzanne said to Neal.

"What do you mean?"

"I could see it in your eyes. You had a confidence about how things would turn out."

Neal appeared to reflect on it a moment. "Faith, I guess."

* * *

Back in his cell, Pierce opened up his Bible and searched through the concordance to find all the references to spiritual gifts. After flipping back and forth for an hour, he looked down at the floor to see a raised ring of dirt in front of his bed. He closed the book, sat up, and brushed over the ring with his foot.

He hoped the tunneling machine was still at work, quietly carving its way down to the next level. From what limited maps and information he had, he knew the vast complex of servers of the Chronopticus Network lie beneath their feet. He imagined himself and Suzanne someday dropping through the floor to run through a maze of monolithic machines.

Chapter Twenty-Four

The following afternoon Pierce was led out of his cell by a Cyclode and a human guard. They travelled down a winding corridor and into a chamber that resembled something out of a medieval painting. Kalen sat before them in a blue velvet and gold-covered chair that sat atop a red-velvet platform with stairs leading up to it. He wore the same Roman outfit he first displayed in public weeks ago and it appeared the only thing missing was a crown. On either side of him stood two cream-colored grooved pillars with lion heads carved into their bases.

Pierce glanced around to see if this room was once a spacious office converted in haste to represent a new seat of power. He smirked at Kalen.

"I suppose you're wondering why I called you in here," Kalen said as he leaned back in his chair. There was an air of arrogance in his voice as if this was all a game to him. "I have to say I was impressed how your little group worked together in the arena. Can't say the same will happen next time, but at least you gave the crowd a good show."

"It wasn't a show."

"Are you saying God saved you? Ooh, can I use that in my next speech?"

Pierce was not amused. "I'm saying there is a lot more at work here than you think."

"Let's not kid ourselves. We all know you use your religion to justify what you do. But when it's taken away, you won't have anything. Then you'll see the light."

"So that's your reeducation plan? Cooperate or be killed?"

Kalen smiled. "Now you're catching on."

"God says no one can snatch those that are His out of His hand. And that He won't leave me or forsake me. Why would I leave Him?"

"You realize I have the power to keep everyone here locked up indefinitely, right? All you have to do is renounce these things and maybe I'll let you out to play."

Pierce did not respond.

Kalen continued. "Or are you waiting for your friends at Camp Io to bail you out? You know there is no Camp Io, right? Io is nothing but a pile of wreckage. We sent a recon scout over there a week ago. There's nothing there. And that loon on the telescreen that's walking around talking to streetlights?" He laughed. "He's an ex-con. Used to smuggle back on Earth and thought he could come up here and set up shop. Saw him coming a mile away. I leave him out there on the streets for entertainment value. A little chaos never hurt the system, right?"

Again, Pierce said nothing. He took a deep breath and could feel sweat on his palms. He knew Kalen was referring to Kyrk, but his own lack of information on the subject did not help his cause.

A wicked smile crossed Kalen's face. "Like it matters anyway. We know what everyone is going to do before they even do it."

"I know someone, too, who has seen everything I've ever done. And it isn't a computer. He knows my thoughts before they are on my tongue. Knows my needs before I even ask. And what's more He knows what you're going to do next because He exists outside of time."

"What is time? Years ago people always talked about time travel. Build a ship, change the future. Change the past. But see, I don't have a need for time travel. My machine can already see through time and I don't have to go anywhere!" Kalen leaned forward and interlaced his fingers as if his patience was wearing thin.

"You're wrong. You can't see into the future."

Kalen climbed down off of his chair and stood right in front of Pierce. His crimson cape flowed out behind him, but there was nothing heroic about his stance. "Oh, but I can. You see, the future is buried in the algorithms of the past. If you know where to look. Remember Countdown? Remember Pastor Capshaw? We knew where he was going to be almost down to the minute. It was so...predictable. But it was more to fun to let everybody else in on the action."

Pierce felt his chest tighten up and his shoulders girded themselves like blocks of iron. "Only God can predict what's going to happen next."

"You just don't give up do you?" Kalen's voice thundered. "I, too, can see from beginning to end. I know what you're planning before you think of it, too. Remember Kayla? I knew she was going to turn on me. We picked it up in her voice patterns. Chronopticus detected subtle changes in the way she addressed me. Same goes for you and Suzanne. I know more about you than you think I do."

Pierce's mind began to race through all their walks down the streets, the times they visited area businesses, and whether Suzanne was being monitored at work. Who knew what her co-workers said behind her back? Then there was the annoying buzz of the busybees.

Kalen began to pace around in circles before him. "If only your friends and co-workers knew who you really were. See, I know all about how you adjusted the budget to fit in your little recon mission to find the five crates. And how you tried to cover it up when things started going wrong. But let's go further back than that."

Pierce remained unmoved but did not like the direction the conversation was heading.

"Let's go back to the time when you first arrived up here. You started out as an architect, right? Then why were you seen making deals with contractors to block the construction of several casinos across the settlements? Were you the one behind Jack Addard's death at the construction site?"

"I had nothing to do with that. That was on Kayla."

Kalen stopped circling and stood before Pierce again. "There's no clear evidence on that. Is it not true that you told several people that if you ran the city, things would be different?"

"I didn't kill Jack."

"Or how about your girlfriend, Suzanne Entner. Did you ever ask her about her past? She really doesn't belong in here. That whole Bible spiel she gave you was just a ruse. She's not really like that. I know the real Suzanne. The one she keeps hidden away from you."

Pierce felt his cheeks become flush. Although his hands were handcuffed behind his back, he struggled against the restraint. "Screw you, Kalen."

Kalen laughed. "Do you even know why I brought you in here?" He motioned to another guard that stood next his regal chair. The guard departed.

A moment later, four human guards entered the chamber. Each man gripped a chain that restrained a strange, metallic creature that had two legs, four arms, and a head like the one found on a mechanical lion. The four men pulled the creature forward so that it stood a few feet in front of Pierce.

"In your next arena match you'll get to meet our first ever Nalwark. He may be a robot in chains but I assure you he's fully autonomous."

Pierce stared the machine in its golden eyes and scoffed. The four arms of the creature writhed about like serpents. At the end of each arm, a four-fingered claw clasped and opened like a spider.

Kalen motioned to the human guard and the Cyclode next to Pierce. "Get him out of here."

As Pierce was escorted out, he fought against the iron grip of the restraints. Just as he was about to pull on his handcuffs and slam the guard into the wall, a thought came into his mind: "Trust Me."

Chapter Twenty-Five

Back in his cell, Pierce stewed in his thoughts for a while before saying a word to Suzanne. He recalled many of the conversations they had over the past few weeks and about how she claimed to have spent time in the Bible while in captivity. Was it all a lie? Although he did not pry too deeply into her past, a cloud of confusion hung over his thoughts and over every word he wanted to say to her. Was her comment that she heard from God just a scam, too? Was Kalen going to move her out of here now that so many people were locked up? Why, then, did Kalen go to the trouble of picking up Suzanne in the first place?

He felt a headache coming on, starting behind his eyes and radiating out further and further as time passed. He spoke up. "Suzanne."

"I'm here. Are you okay?"

He opened up his Bible to the Book of James and skimmed the text. "When you said you spent time in your cell reading the Bible, did you read the part in James where he talks about speaking in tongues?"

"James doesn't talk about speaking in tongues. He talks about the tongue, but that's different. You're thinking of First Corinthians."

"Yeah, but over in the Book of Hezekiah it talks about it, too."

Suzanne laughed quietly. "There is no Book of Hezekiah."

"Sure there is. It's next to the Book of Amos."

"Uh-huh. And what's on the other side of that? The Book of Andy? You sure you're okay over there? Kalen didn't slip something in your drink did he?"

Pierce smiled to himself. "No, but he tried to intimidate me. Told me he knew everything about your past and mine."

"Really." The sarcasm in her voice was thick. "What did he say about me?"

"He says your faith is all a ruse."

Suzanne remained silent.

"It's not is it?"

"Hardly."

As he closed his book the walls of his cell shook violently. The lights flickered as more dirt rained down on top of him. He jumped off the bed and stood in the middle of his cell until the shaking stopped. He walked over to his cell door and tried to push it open but it did not budge. Now he knew this was not the result of a tunneling operation and if the complex collapsed in a quake, he hoped they would have time enough to escape.

"You okay, Suzanne?"

"I'm fine. But I hope the quakes don't get worse. We might not make it out alive."

"Know what else Kalen said to me back there? He said his time machine sees everything. Even into the future."

"So now he's a time traveler? Get real."

"I think he thinks he is judge and executioner all in one."

"God's the real judge," Anyk said from across the hallway.

Pierce turned and nodded toward Anyk. He often wondered what it would be like to overhaul the legal system here, since the executives back on Earth practically wrote all the rules, enforced them, and then jailed troublemakers without a trial.

Anyk continued. "That must have been how they found me. It was like the Cyclodes knew I was going to be at my brother's house and they showed up a minute before I got there. My brother tried to warn me, but when I turned my car around they surrounded me and carted me off."

Pierce flipped to the back of his Bible and found several blank pages. He stared at them a moment and then had an idea. He tore the blank pages out and dug out a short stub of a pencil that he brought inside of his uniform on the day of his capture. There was not much left to the pencil, but there was enough lead to write a few notes. He began to scribble down a few ideas for an escape plan along with a diagram. When he finished, he folded the paper into eighths and walked over to the edge of his cell. He looked down at his badge and noticed it was still bright red.

He stuck his arm out through the bars and pitched the paper in front of Suzanne's cell. "Psst," he said. "Give me your thoughts on this."

She reached out and picked up the note. "Do you have something to write with?" She said.

He took the pencil stub and threw that in front of her cell. When she finished, she threw everything back.

He retrieved the note and unfolded it. It read: "Good plan. But once we get in the server room, then what?"

He thought about this a moment and knew he did not have a map of the server room below them. Who knew how many escape routes led out of there, how many guards there were, or if there were electronic surveillance devices in place to track their every move. As he sat next to the bars of his cell, he stared again at the faint circle on the floor. Who knew if the tunneling die was still at work or if it ran out of power? Was the machine cutting through rock and steel? Maybe they should all start an argument in the cafeteria and in the confusion make a break for it.

He flipped the paper over and began to write again. Once in the server room, he wrote, they could figure out how to open the cell locks on the floor above and then take the system offline. In the confusion, they could make a run for the crawler dock and race back toward Magnopolis.

He folded up the note. He turned back toward the hallway, pitched the note toward Suzanne's cell, and waited.

Chapter Twenty-Six

Pierce awoke out of his slumber to the sounds of shouting guards. He could hear a female prisoner being interrogated and threats being made. He rolled out of bed and walked over to the edge of his cell.

Anyk waved at him from across the aisle. "Ryan and Ruelle are gone," he whispered just beneath the shouts from the down the hallway.

"They took them away?"

Anyk shook his head from side to side and smiled. He extended his arm and made a circular motion with his index finger pointed toward the floor.

At that moment, Pierce felt a strange sense of calm as if someone was praying for him. He felt a surge of courage and peace unlike anything he had ever experienced. His thoughts flashed back to Ryan kneeling down in the arena to heal Lynn when she was mauled by the mechanical lion. He remembered how Ruelle prayed while she was being hauled away in front of the Network news cameras.

As he pressed his face to the bars to try to get a better look at the commotion down the hallway, he heard a rustling in Suzanne's cell. He saw her reach out of her cell and pitch a folded-up piece of paper back in front of him. In haste, he knelt down and pulled it into his cell before anyone would notice.

He read the note silently to himself. "I passed this note down the line. See their notes below. Read Omar's note."

He scanned the page for what looked like Omar's slanted handwriting. It read: "Kyrk and I flooded the Network with junk data. Camp Io is real. It's the wreckage of Ionotatron. The Sentinels will try to march on it. If they attack it, it will take them out."

Pierce puzzled over the last comment since Io had been disabled for some time and was nothing more than a pile of metal and electronics being buried by the Martian sands of time. As the guards continued to shout and interrogate the prisoners around Ruelle and Ryan's cells, he wondered how much longer it would be before he, Anyk, and Suzanne crashed through the floor and disappeared.

Soon the commotion in the hallway ceased. He closed his eyes, folded his hands, and tried to dream of the last fishing trip he took back on Earth with his friends. It was a night of unparalleled walleye fishing, with fourteen to sixteen inch fish coming into the boat one after the other. Although they released most of the fish, they kept the last few for dinner. From the zing of his reel to the poke of a dorsal fin on the palm of his hand to the scent of frying oil and Cajun seasonings afterward, some memories were so etched in his mind that it was as if he could reach back into yesterday and touch them.

Chapter Twenty-Seven

Pierce slept a few more hours before he heard a thunderous crash in the cell next to him. He sprang out of bed and to his feet. Across the aisle, Anyk jumped up and down in the middle of the cell and waved at Pierce. He gave Pierce a thumbs-up sign before the floor gave way.

In shock, Pierce watched Anyk disappear along with a chunk of the floor to the level below. He was sure the guards would be back in an instant. He stood inside the ring in his own cell. With nothing to lose, he jumped up and down and hoped for the best.

Down the hallway he heard shouts and then another crash that was louder than the first. He jumped up and down harder and then looked up toward the ceiling. In frustration, he sat down on the floor and put his head into his hands.

At that, he felt a trembling underneath him. He opened his eyes and soon his stomach leapt up into his chest. He found himself in a freefall and spread out his arms in desperation. The fall was only a few feet, but it nearly knocked him unconscious as the disc of flooring material hit the top of a server rack and wobbled toward the floor.

He braced himself for impact. He clutched the back of one of the server racks and took a dozen cables with him as he hit the floor. When the dust cleared and he regained his senses, he saw Suzanne and Anyk standing over him. Omar and Lynn Goldman rushed up to his side a minute later.

"We have to get going. It won't be long before they find out we're down here," Omar said while lending Pierce a hand.

Pierce stood up. Half out of it from the fall, he took a deep breath. Up above he could hear more shouts and soon a couple of ion coil pistol rounds were fired through the new holes in the ceiling. One of the server towers where Pierce crashed through the floor began to smolder.

"Where do we go from here?" Suzanne asked.

"I think we can head down this way," Omar said, pointing ahead of them toward a hallway. To the left, right, and all around them were six-foot high, black, monolithic banks of computers with a minimal amount of cables running between them. The banks of computers stretched on forever in all directions like an endless maze of Dominoes.

"How do we get the others out?" Pierce said as he motioned toward the ceiling.

"I have an idea," Omar replied.

"What did you mean up there when you said that if the Cyclodes attack Io it will take them out?"

Omar smiled. "Kyrk is back in town flooding the system with junk data. Put enough into the system and it'll go into overload. They'll become obsessed with Camp Io and then..."

Pierce waited for him to finish his sentence.

"...then if they fire on it, it'll explode."

"But there's nothing left to Io's electronics. It's a dead machine."

Omar smiled again. "It's not as dead as you think."

"You mean we didn't really take it down?"

"You did that. But there's a doomsday device onboard."

"Built into it?"

"No. Put there by some crazy guy who talks to streetlights."

Just then, Pierce saw an ion coil round fly through one of the holes in the ceiling and hit the floor right behind them. The impact threw up a plume of dust. All five of them went into a sprint with Omar leading the way. More rounds pummeled the floor behind them and he knew it could only be minutes before a Cyclode Sentinel was dropped through one of the holes or sent down here in the elevators.

As they wove their way through the maze of monoliths, he wondered if they should be following the same pattern than Neal suggested when they were being pursued by the lions in the Coliseum. When they passed by a lone computer terminal along one of the walkways, Omar stopped and looked back at the machine.

Omar sat down at the machine and activated it. In seconds the terminal screen flashed a set of logos and instructions and he busily began typing in a chain of commands.

"What are you doing?" Lynn shouted.

Omar held up a hand toward his wife. "Give me five minutes. Just five."

"We don't have five minutes."

"Okay, two."

Chapter Twenty-Eight

"They're not going to like me for this," Omar said as he hammered away at the keyboard. He stopped and looked back at Pierce, then at Suzanne.

"What?" Pierce said.

"I'm in, but I don't have the password to release the cell doors."

In the distance, Pierce could hear the motors of the elevators going up and down between floors. He knew their time was dwindling and they still had not figured out a way out of the server maze.

Omar turned back toward the machine and tried a few phrases. None of them worked. In frustration, he threw his hands up in the air.

Suzanne moved over toward the screen. "What's it asking you for? Does it give you any hints?"

"It says timebird. I don't know what a timebird is. It keeps asking me for a passphrase."

Pierce drew back. "What's a timebird?"

Lynn closed in and stared hard at the screen.

Omar turned to her. "What is it?"

"Strange. There's Latin writing on the background of the page."

"So what's Latin for bird?"

"Try avis."

He typed the word and the system rejected it.

"Try aves. That's for more than one bird."

The system still rejected it.

"Wait. What do birds do?" Pierce said.

"They fly," Anyk added.

"So Latinfly?" Omar said. He tried the phrase. No dice.

"Try night owl," Pierce suggested. That did not work either.

Suzanne crossed her arms. "My uncle used to have this clock in his house back on Earth. I'm trying to remember what it said on the face of the clock. Something about flying."

"Time flies," Pierce said.

"What? Time flies. Okay." Omar typed it into the terminal. It still did not let him past.

"Try tempus fugit," Lynn said with a smile.

Omar typed the phrase and the machine complied. A new screen appeared which displayed a map of the upstairs level. On the map the cell doors were represented by thin red bars. After a few quick keystrokes, the red bars disappeared.

He turned back to face them with a smile. He motioned toward a door just down the hallway from them. "Let's go." He stood up and grabbed Lynn's hand.

Meanwhile, Pierce sat down at the terminal. He pecked away at the keyboard and changed to a different system via the menu at the top of the screen.

"What are you doing?" Suzanne said as she tugged on his shirt sleeve.

"Hang on, I have to see something." He worked his way through several screens, learning how to navigate them on the fly. He was impressed by the amount of information he had at his fingertips and longed to download it all into a portable storage device. He looked around on the desk and pulled open the drawer. Inside was a video plate.

He plugged the plate into a slot in the terminal and started typing again. Soon, he found himself on a screen that revealed histories of those inside of the Dexler Corporation, including profiles of Kayla and Kalen Rusk.

Suzanne pulled at his shirt harder. "They're coming for us. C'mon. We're going to get left behind."

He could hear the cyclic crunch-crunch of Cyclode Sentinel machinery down a distant hallway and knew he only had mere seconds left. He downloaded the profile for Kayla and then for Kalen, along with a handful of other people. He tapped a few more keys, exited out of the system, and stuffed the video plate in his pants pocket.

As they ran toward the exit, Pierce felt like they were running through a maze of people's identities, secrets, and dreams. The power at his fingertips moments ago was intoxicating and revolting at the same time. He relished the thought of being able to predict Kalen's next moves, but like the passphrase on the terminal screen, he knew that the time to act was quickly fleeing from him.

* * *

By the time they reached the crawler dock, all of them were winded from the run. They found a few pressure suits hanging on the wall and slipped them on in haste. Pierce checked over a nearby crawler to see if it was equipped with weapons. Seeing a lone ion coil cannon on the roof of the crawler, he winced but knew they had to take what they could get at this point.

Omar took over the driver's seat while the rest of them piled into the machine. He popped off the panel on the side of the steering column and tinkered with the wires, much like James did with the monowheels. In under a minute, the main door was closed. Lynn activated the airlock controls and Omar got the engine going. They rode up an elongated tunnel which ran back up toward the desert surface.

Pierce relaxed as it was the first sunlight he had seen in days. In celebration, he gave Suzanne a kiss flush on the lips.

Lynn reached over to activate the console telescreen in the front of the cockpit. Pierce and Suzanne leaned in to see what information was coming back on the radar screen and another screen which displayed a news channel. Although the news channel was muted, Pierce could see maps and images of the recent quakes in the region and it became clear to him something was wrong underneath the mountain range they were now leaving behind.

Anyk became restless in his seat.

"What is it?" Omar asked, looking up.

"Someone should man the gun," Anyk said. He moved toward the middle of the vehicle and activated the cannon system. He then settled down into the rotating chair and pulled down a weapons control screen. Next, he grabbed a hold of the trigger stick that controlled the cannon.

Pierce watched as Anyk familiarized himself with the controls. Pierce turned back to look out of a side window. The landscape came alive for him with features he did not notice before today, such as new dust devil trails and the windswept remains of an ancient riverbed. He wondered if anybody had ever dug through the thirsty ground in search of fossils.

"Incoming," Anyk said suddenly.

Pierce leaned over to look at the weapons control screen. Four objects moved out of and away from the Chronopticus mountain complex with a bearing on their vehicle. He had no way of knowing if they were Cyclodes or crawlers. If they were crawlers, he could not tell if they were friendly or of enemy origin.

Anyk switched to a camera view. "I've got a visual on our pursuers. Looks like four Cyclodes. Might be able to outrun them if we gun it."

"Gun it," Lynn said as she motioned toward Omar.

"I'm trying!" Omar replied, shaking his head.

Ion coil rounds slammed into the ground on either side of the crawler and forced Omar to swerve to avoid getting hit. Anyk wheeled around and fired back.

One of the dots disappeared off the radar. The rounds flew in with greater frequency. Again, Anyk fired back. A round hit the side of their crawler and knocked them off course by a few feet.

Pierce watched as the three remaining objects on the radar blinked out one by one. "Nice work, Anyk," he said as he leaned over and patted him on the back.

"It wasn't me."

Pierce looked back at the radar and saw two more objects appear. The objects were amber in color and not red.

Suzanne pointed out the window toward a pair of crawlers rolling on the sand behind them. "Looks like help is on the way."

Chapter Twenty-Nine

By the time they arrived back in Magnopolis, Pierce figured there would again be no hero's welcome, but rather riots. Instead, the city was quiet. Suzanne first headed over to her sister Lisabeth's house and Pierce headed home. Both knew their risk of being reacquired was astronomically high, but they agreed they needed to find James and then regroup to figure out what to do next.

As Pierce raced down the street, he detected movement out of the corner of his eye. At first, he thought it was a Cyclode. When he turned to look, he saw nothing unusual in the neighborhood. The hair on his arms stood on end. He looked up to see if any busybees were hovering near the rooftops. Seeing nothing unusual, he pressed on, but at a quicker pace.

Just as he rounded the final corner near his home, he heard an electric car pull up behind him. He did not want to turn around. He slowed his pace to a walk and stuffed his hands into his pants pockets. A black car pulled ahead of him and next to the curb before coming to a stop.

Kalen stepped out of the passenger side of the vehicle, dressed in his bizarre Roman outfit, and waited for Pierce on the sidewalk. Pierce thought for sure that Kalen would have pulled up in a custom-made electric chariot. He also knew the Cyclodes could not be far behind and he wondered if he would ever set foot in his own home again.

Kalen smiled. "See what I mean? I know where you're going before you even arrive. Technically, I can order any Cyclode to strike you down right here."

"Why? I'm already dead. Besides, if you take me out, do you know where I go? You still have time to turn around."

Kalen replied with a hearty laugh. "Why doesn't your God manifest Himself before me?"

Pierce did not have an immediate reply. Then, a phrase came into his mind. "Psalm 23," he said out loud.

"What?" Kalen looked back toward the electric car and motioned to the driver. The driver reached over onto the dashboard and picked up a video plate. He leaned over across the passenger seat and handed it over to Kalen.

As Kalen moved through different screens on his device, he became irritated.

"Something wrong?" Pierce said.

Kalen did not reply.

"It's not there is it? Your workers had it removed. It was a dangerous book you once said." Pierce looked around the neighborhood and then bore down on Kalen with his eyes. "It says in there that Heaven and Earth will pass away but His words will never pass away."

Kalen handed the video plate back to the driver. "We're not on Earth, Steadman. Oh, and I sent out some Sentinels to go and check on your Camp Io. If there is anything there, it'll be gone by daybreak."

Pierce was unmoved. "Help me understand something. Your system...it collects all kinds of data, right?"

"Right," Kalen said with a smug look on his face.

"So how do you sort out the truth from the lies?"

"The inconsistencies get picked up by our algorithms."

"What if a lie is consistent and repeated? Does that make it true? Come now, let us reason together."

Kalen shifted his feet nervously. He looked to the side and then gave Pierce his fiercest look yet. "It can pick up on that, too."

"What about bad data? What about the people under you? Or do you just employ people and programs to alter the data and twist it to suit your dark purposes? What if those people are just as corrupt as you are?"

"Clever. Like I said, I can see their schemes a mile away. I take them out before they ever become a problem."

"Like Kayla? She was loyal to you even near the end. In fact, her file says she was a code yellow at best. You just thought it was convenient to take her out." Although Pierce had not seen the data on the video plate from the server room, he was pretty sure of its contents.

"Is your God going to answer me or what? I'm a busy man."

Kalen leaned back through the window of the electric car and said something to the driver. The driver reached over and pressed a few buttons on the console dashboard.

Pierce knew the Cyclodes would close on him any minute now. Would Kalen let him run this time? Did Kalen know the extent of the jailbreak at the Complex? Pierce began to run toward his house.

"Go ahead. Run. There's no where you can go anyway. Or are you waiting for God to save you? Do you see how narrow that is?"

Pierce looked back. "It may be narrow, but it's narrow for a good reason."

Just then, the driver called out to Kalen. Kalen leaned in through the car window again and then backed away. He opened the passenger door and briefly stared at something behind Pierce. He gave Pierce one last grin before climbing into the car.

Pierce turned around to see a mechanized Nalwark as it walked down the street toward him. This time, there were no chains of restraint and each arm wielded a short sword. Kalen's black car sped off with a squeal of the tires.

As the machine approached, all four of its arms began to spin. The swords became a blur, as if there were four circular saw blades coming at him from different directions. Pierce knew the creature could outrun him and he doubted running in a zigzag pattern would do any good.

As he backed up, he searched the ground and neighboring yards for any kind of weapon that would buy him time. The Nalwark increased its forward speed as if it wanted Pierce to go into a run.

He darted behind a small tree whose top was a few feet above his head. The Nalwark lunged at him and took a swipe at the tree. The leaves on the tree were shredded as he ducked out of the way. With one swing the machine sliced the tree in half.

Pierce ran full speed toward a yard and jetted in between two houses. On the way through he picked up a handful of bright blue decorative rocks and threw it back at the machine. Without effect the whirling swords sent the rocks ricocheting back at him.

The Nalwark took another swing at his head. It missed and two of the swords plunged into the side of a house, taking pieces of siding with it.

Stunned, the machine stopped to pull its swords out. Pierce scampered through another yard and dove behind some playground equipment. The Nalwark followed and struck at him repeatedly. Blow after blow missed and hit the monkey bars, the metal slide, and then a steel rung ladder. Sparks flew. Metal clashed against metal as Pierce rolled and weaved about.

As the playground fell into pieces he sprinted toward a chain-link fence. The Nalwark followed. He scaled the fence and dropped to the other side. The Nalwark kicked the fence in as he stumbled to the ground.

The machine swung first at his legs and then at his head. Just as the Nalwark swung at his arms he saw two chains fly in from opposite sides and wrap themselves around two different arms of the machine. Before the Nalwark could react the arms flew off in separate directions. The Nalwark spun around with wires hanging from its arm sockets.

Seconds later the machine convulsed under waves of ion coil pistol fire. The machine jerked about, dropped into a heap, and smoked. As Pierce sat up, Ryan and Ruelle came over to help him to his feet.

Chapter Thirty

When Pierce finally made it home, he checked on his belongings. The house appeared untouched. He looked back out the front window, then poked his head out the front door and listened. In the distance, he heard a siren and the scent of plastic smoke tainted the air. He saw a swarm of busybees flying in a cloud formation toward downtown. The swarm cast a shadow across his yard and then up the street.

He crept out into the street and headed to Suzanne's house. In theory, he reasoned, she should be back from Lisabeth's house by now. He took an offbeat route to her house that avoided the downtown area. As he passed downtown, he looked over to see the giant hourglass in Meres Park was broken in several places. Blood red dust had spilled out into the street and street sweepers were out cleaning up the mess.

When he arrived at Suzanne's house, he found Omar and Lynn there in the living room. All of them were gathered around the telescreen and watched Kalen as he ended an emergency speech.

"What's going on?" He asked as he stood next to Suzanne.

James ran up to him and python-hugged his leg. "Dad!" He said without hesitation.

"I missed you, too, son." It was a risky and awkward word to use at first, but he had a feeling with time it might get easier. James hugged him tighter.

Pierce looked on at Suzanne and then back at James. "I couldn't stop worrying about you. Are you okay?"

"I'm great."

"Any bruises? Scratches?"

The boy shook his head no. Suzanne grabbed a hold of Pierce's hand and pulled him down toward the sofa.

"You missed the panic speech," Omar said. "Or that's what it sounded like to me. Kalen's losing control."

"How so?"

"First he talked about the prison break at the Complex. Then he talked about cracking down on the vandals. Someone even hit the casino with nanoparticle graffiti. Remember that stupid hourglass they had in downtown? Someone broke it."

"I saw that," Pierce said with a smile.

"But his speech was cut short. One of the Cyclodes in the background went go out of control. So they cut the camera feed."

For the first time in weeks, Pierce felt a measure of hope surge inside of him. "Just one? Or are there more?"

Omar leaned back and chuckled. "Remember the upgrades we did?"

Pierce nodded.

"I put a piece of code in there that would be triggered by a certain command. Sort of like a kill switch. Only it didn't work right at first. I didn't get time to test it further, but Kyrk has been testing it."

"By talking to streetlights?"

"Yes."

"Can I ask what the command was?"

Omar put his hands behind his neck. "Seize Io."

"Did he test it tonight?"

"Yes. If it works, Kalen will gradually lose control of the Cyclodes. They'll all get caught up in a race condition."

Pierce walked over to the living room window. He pulled aside one of the burgundy curtains to peer down the street. He saw a man running by with a Cyclode in pursuit, but it was not Kyrk. In the distance a column of black smoke rose up.

"What happens during the race condition?" Suzanne asked.

"They generally home in on a single target. And lock up one by one," Omar said.

"In other words, an Entner collision," Pierce added.

Suzanne stood up and brushed her hand against Pierce's cheek. "What happened to you by the way? You look like you were in a street fight."

"I was. Ruelle and Ryan helped me fight off a Nalwark." He looked down and discovered a tear in his shirt where his food badge used to be. Then he saw the bottom of his pants had been slashed. He pulled back the pant leg and found a bloody scrape on his ankle.

Suzanne knelt down and examined his ankle wound. "What's a Nalwark?"

"Four swords. Spinning arms. Fully automated." He made an exaggerated gesture with his hands to try and indicate its size. "Probably about this big."

Suzanne's eyes widened.

"Oh, don't worry. It was one of a kind."

Chapter Thirty-One

Omar switched the telescreen to a map of the recent quakes in the area. "And check this out. There has been a huge swarm of mini-quakes near the prison complex."

"The Network has been really unstable today," Suzanne noted. "Think it's related?"

The lights flickered. Soon, the power went out. The house shook and several pictures fell down off the walls. A floor lamp toppled over and plates poured out of the cupboards in the kitchen and crashed to the floor. Lynn screamed.

Pierce looked out the front window. Other homes in the neighborhood were dark and a streetlight across the way fell into the street. When the shaking stopped, he spoke up. "So what happens if the Network gets completely unstable?"

"Who knows. The Cyclodes may go into autonomous mode," Omar said.

"Meaning what?"

"Meaning they'll draw on whatever data is available in the Network for a person." Omar hesitated before commenting further. It was as if he did not want to outline any more possibilities.

"In other words Kalen's lost all control over the Network," Pierce said.

Omar shook his head in affirmation. Suzanne went into the kitchen to check the fuse box but came back with downcast eyes. The power came back up a minute later, but who knew how long that would last. Suzanne began to light a few tea candles.

"Can we see what happened?" James said excitedly.

Pierce nodded and led the boy outside. In the distance, toward the direction of the Chronopticus Complex, he could see smoke rising. He motioned for James to go back inside. "Let's grab our suits and go for a ride."

"Just you and me?"

"Just you and me."

"Where are you going?" Suzanne said with her hands on her hips.

"Out for a ride," Pierce replied.

"But you don't know what happened out there. It could be dangerous."

Pierce gave her a wink. "I'm not worried. Trust me."

* * *

Pierce and James drove out of the crawler dock and toward the Chronopticus Network complex. Although the ground shook a handful of times on their voyage, the tremors were smaller than any of the previous ones. As Pierce rolled toward the mountain, he scouted out a ridge where they could get a better view. Upon parking the vehicle, he spoke up.

"See all that?" He pointed toward a column of black smoke and steam that vented from the mountain side. "That's a dormant volcano come to life."

James watched on in awe. "Is there any lava?"

"I don't see any, but I'm sure there is some. Someday when this has all blown over I'll take you out there and show the lava tubes."

The boy beamed.

"Dad? I mean, Pierce?"

"Yes?"

"Are you going to marry my Mom?"

Pierce gave him a huge smile.

"Because if you are," James continued, "I want to go on more crawler rides. Mom doesn't like crawler rides anymore."

"Okay, we can go on more crawler rides."

"Oh, and can I have a telescreen in my room? Mom won't let me have one of those."

"Okay. I'll talk to her about it."

"Oh, and can we order pizza at least once a week? I really like pizza."

Chapter Thirty-Two

By the time Pierce and James returned to the house, the telescreen was still on the fritz. Updates became infrequent on the Network and several times the picture froze. The pictures that did appear caught everyone in the room by surprise. There, on the screen, were images of the Chronopticus Network mountain complex with thick, black, smoke and steam pouring out of it. Although no fire could be seen, it was clear that one was burning internally.

Across the bottom of the screen scrolled a headline that Pierce never thought he would see: "Volcanic explosion likely at mountain complex…lava seen pouring out of entrance to facility…Kalen Rusk, CEO of Dexler Corporation, likely among the fatalities."

"Time's up," Omar said, echoing the phrase that was popularized by a telescreen announcer at the end of each endeavor.

"Do you think he even had a chance?" Suzanne said as she watched on.

"Considering the way the Network was acting up this morning…no. If the explosion didn't take him out, his own machines would have," Pierce said.

"Pierce, come check this out," Omar called out as he held a video plate in his hands.

Pierce, James, and Suzanne ran over to him, where Omar and Lynn focused intently on the screen. Omar pointed to the screen.

"With all of the Network chaos, I was able to tap into the Cyclode camera system. I don't know how long this feed will last. But it looks like they are headed somewhere in a group," Omar said.

"To the mountain base?"

"No. They're moving toward a point in front of it. I think they're heading for Io. Here, let me project it onto the telescreen."

Pierce watched as the images streamed in. The images were often scrambled by static or froze for seconds at a time. By the looks of the formation, a few dozen Cyclodes were on a march toward the remnants of Io. Hundreds of yards ahead, he could see the faint outlines of the half-covered giant machine as it lay face down in the dust. The machine looked as if it was in a perpetual state of clawing its way out of the sand.

Gradually, Io's immense figure came into focus. Then the Cyclode with the camera feed stopped in its tracks. The remaining machines also stopped and encircled the fallen relic of Io.

"Seize Io," Omar said with a smile.

Round after round of ion coil fire flew into Io from all directions. Then came a bright burst of light from Io itself and finally darkness. The image stream went black.

A smile broke across all of their faces. The lights flickered again in the house and then stayed on.

Suzanne faced Pierce. "About those profiles you downloaded back in the server room. What was in them?"

Pierce grinned. "Let me show you." He withdrew the server room video plate from his pocket and turned it on. Dozens of names had been downloaded onto the device. As he scrolled through the list of names he came across profiles for Kayla, Kalen, Suzanne, Pastor Capshaw, and himself. He stared at the screen, hypnotized by what he read.

"Pierce? Are you okay?" Suzanne said.

Pierce nodded and read through the profile for Kayla, Jack Addard's former assistant. "Listen to this. The system says Kayla did not present a threat. If she would have had a badge color it would have been light yellow at worst. She was loyal to the end."

"But then why did Kalen have her killed?"

"He claimed it had something to do with her speech patterns." Pierce flipped to the page that analyzed her speech patterns over time. The system noted nothing unusual beyond routine stress, except right at the end of her life.

He was surprised by the incredible amount of data analyzed by the system. The data included visual images, sound recordings, Network interaction history, and location data. The deepest detail was found after a person ended up on Mars with their Earth history, if applicable, summarized by a few paragraphs. The data could be sorted by time or subject and each profile contained information that included future projections of a person's behavior.

Pierce looked up. "I think he just chose to pick her off and lied about the speech patterns. Unless there was something in her Earth profile that bugged him." He showed the plate to Suzanne.

"Look up Kalen's profile," she said as Pierce changed screens.

"Shows him as being the least threat on the Network up until the other day."

"What happened the other day?" Omar asked, as he leaned over to see the video plate.

"Says here his badge color was white up until the day he confronted me in prison. Then it started turning color." Pierce looked up. "I wonder if he tried looking up something and the system perceived him as a threat. Either that or it saw him as having too much authority."

"You mean like a power struggle between him and the Network computers?" Suzanne asked.

Pierce nodded. "Funny. On my profile it says I was a threat to sabotage City Hall and the Towers of Venice casino. The graphs said I would have taken one of the buildings down in the next two weeks."

"Would you have?" Lynn asked.

"No. I was never interested in that. I also wasn't interested in building more casinos. There were a lot of contractors who agreed with me."

Pierce continued to scroll through the screens. He came upon Suzanne's profile. "What's the Dove League?"

"Where does it say that? Whose profile is that?" Suzanne asked as she inched toward him. She tried to grab the plate out of his hands, but he tightened his grip.

"Says you were a member for years. But you stopped attending meetings part way into your time here. Just after you met me."

Pierce looked up as Suzanne looked away and toward the floor. Her cheeks became flush.

"What was it?" He repeated.

"An anti-religious organization. I'm not proud of it, though. And I haven't talked with them in years. I don't want to go back to them ever again."

"They are a group that undermines the churches. Not too many of them up here, but more of them live back on Earth," Omar added.

"They're responsible for the slogan of 'Peace Through Reeducation.'"

Pierce recalled all the Dove League posters he saw scattered around the settlements over the past few months. There must have been some connection between them and Kalen since they used similar terminology, or at least they borrowed from one another. He then read about the loss of Suzanne's husband, her failed attempt to start a widow's support group, and her love for puppies.

Suzanne reached for the video plate again and this time Pierce let her have it. "You're obsessed with this thing," she said.

"It's kind of like a time machine." He reached back for the plate but this time Suzanne did not let go. "Seriously. Where do you want to go. Look, you can pick out which day, month, and year right here." He pointed to a menu on the tiny screen.

She started to stare at the screen just as Pierce did earlier. She flipped through profile after profile at lightning speed.

"So where do you want to go?" Pierce said again.

Suzanne looked around the room at the others. A frown swept across her face. "Let's break this thing in half."

"What? Are you kidding?" As soon as the words escaped his lips, he regretted it. He knew deep down she was right and in the wrong hands even this miniature version of the Network time machine was probably going to create more problems.

She held the plate out to him as if it was a wishbone and looked up at him with somber eyes. With reluctance, he grabbed the other side of it. Together they snapped it in half. The screen went black.

"Maybe a little mystery is a good thing," he said after a moment.

Suzanne stared deep into his eyes and held up her half of the broken video plate. "Here's to mystery."

He lifted up his half of the plate. "To mystery."

Chapter Thirty-Three

Pierce knelt down next to the trap door in the middle of the street and pried his fingers underneath it. With a sharp jerk it lifted up. A thin curtain of dust fell down from its edges into the darkness below. He shone his flashlight down the stairs and swept the beam from side to side.

Seeing nothing, he stepped down the stairs and into the tunnel system which ran underneath the city. As he scanned about in the darkness, he truly wondered if the danger had passed. There were still sporadic reports of Cyclodes taking random shots at citizens, but so many of them had been eliminated in the quest to destroy the mythical Camp Io that the remaining few left on the force were deactivated by all possible means.

As he crept along, he searched for his lost notebook of futuristic city plans. *Maybe it was a foolish pursuit*, he thought, *in light of all that has happened to us.* The further he walked through the tunnels, the more he began to lose heart that someone else had come along and taken the notebook or disposed of it in the city dump. Who knew if the notebook was still intact or if the pages were strewn about throughout the tunnels?

At the junction of another tunnel, he spotted a flash of white. He paced up to it and reached down to pick up his notebook. He put the flashlight under his arm and leafed through the pages. The cover was gone, but it did not matter. Finding no pages missing, he clenched the notebook tight and headed back up to the street level.

Although the notebook was frayed around the edges the designs inside remained untouched. Yet the moment was bittersweet at best. He knew his priorities had changed since the last time he held the notebook and, like so many other things in his life, he stopped placing it above God.

As his fingers ran along the tattered paper edges, he sensed his own frailty and looked toward the domed sky. "Thanks," he said without caring who was listening. "But now what do I do?"

As he shut the trap door behind him, dazed citizens came out of their homes one by one. First, it was on Cantor Street. Then doors opened on the other streets. Some of the people he passed looked as if they had just awoken from a long slumber. Although he could still see lights on in the neighborhood, he knew that even the backup Network system had likely failed at last. *Maybe that was a good thing*, he thought to himself.

As he returned home, a male voice called out from behind him. He turned around to see the mechanic that he met in the Chinese restaurant months ago. He extended a hand to shake. "Thanks for saving us," Pierce said as he tucked his notebook under the other arm.

"Anytime. Any chance of you becoming mayor again? I'd vote for you," the mechanic said.

"I thought you didn't agree with me."

"I don't. On some things. But I still think you're the right guy. Better than that other clown that ran this place into the ground."

Pierce smiled but still felt uneasy. "Who says I can do a better job?"

"Yeah, but look at what you already did. You stopped the attacks. Then I saw you on the telescreen taking down lions. Who put you up to that anyway?"

"The last mayor."

The mechanic began to walk away. "Yeah, well, you've got my vote to be the next one."

The more Pierce thought about it, the more he wondered if he should step back into the role if it was offered to him. "What's your name, by the way?"

"Dave. Dave Epson."

"Glad we could talk again, Dave. Maybe you'll get your chance to vote soon. The deputy mayor position was never filled again after I left anyway."

Pierce turned to walk toward his house again. Before he could make it to the front door, he heard a whirring sound high above and to the right of him. He looked up to see a busybee tumbling toward him in a corkscrew motion. He ducked out of the way as the device hit the sidewalk and fell silent. Soon, a swarm of busybees fell out of the heavens and tapped the street like black raindrops.

He reached down to pick up one of them and studied its body. The device remained dead and a small part of him rejoiced. The entire time machine of the Network finally ground to a halt. The city would be forced to deal with life in the present instead of obsessing over the static past and the algorithmic false prophecies of the future. Peace through reeducation just might come to pass, he reasoned, but not the way the Eden Project's founders intended.

He pocketed the busybee and then picked up a few more in the final stretch of sidewalk in front of his house. James was bound to find something fascinating about them.

Chapter Thirty-Four

With the mayoral position vacated by Kalen's death and the deputy mayor never replaced, the city of Magnopolis held an emergency election. Despite members of the City Council running for the position, Pierce won the race by a landslide. The next closest candidate, Arielle Warzecha, came in a distant second with four percent of the votes.

Pierce eased himself into the office chair that he was forcibly removed from only a few weeks ago. The City Council members, Arielle, Isaac Parker, and Melinda Jacobson filed in one by one and sat in the semicircle of chairs before his desk. Arielle was the still the head of Human Resources, Accounting, and Legal, Isaac was still in charge of Public Works and Transportation, and Melinda oversaw Parks and Planning. Arielle set a holographic video recording device on the edge of Pierce's desk and pressed a black button on the top of the device to activate it.

Pierce cleared his throat and tried to keep a straight face. "The first thing I would like to cover is the remodeling of this office. All this..." He gestured toward the two faux marble pillars behind his desk and then toward the gold-leaf trim along the walls. "...has to go. This isn't Rome. I can't believe you put up with this."

Arielle cleared her throat but did not look him in the eye. "That's not fair. You know we'd had no..."

"No what? No choice? Shall we talk about fair? Do you think it was fair that I went off to a lion pit and you got to sit back and watch it all from your office?"

None of the council members stirred.

"So let's vote on this. All of those in favor of removing the Roman Empire decorations say yay."

All of them agreed.

"Let's also throw out the badge system. In fact, I'll be the first to participate." Pierce reached down and tore the food badge off his shirt and dropped it into the trash. It was Suzanne's old badge and he had put it on as a joke before he left the house for the day. The others still kept their badges visible on their shirts. All of their badges were colored black due to the ongoing Network outage. "All of those in favor say..."

"Wait. What are we going to replace it with? The ag domes still have not fully recovered. We're only back up to ninety percent capacity," Melinda said.

"That's not what the news said before the Network outage."

Arielle rolled her eyes.

Pierce continued. "My suggestion is that we don't replace them with anything, if that answers your question. All of those in favor say..."

"But what about enforcement?" Isaac said. "Don't we still need the badges to sort out..."

"Sort out what? Or do you enjoy having a window into other people's private lives? How about this. Either the badges go or I go."

The room fell silent. Pierce looked over at Arielle and he could tell she actually relished the thought. "Maybe this whole board should be overturned," he said after a pause.

That comment brought a chorus of rejections that Pierce shot down one by one. "Let's try this again. Badge system, yay or nay."

The group agreed on retiring it after further rounds of vigorous debate. The meeting carried on until Pierce reached over and turned off the holographic recorder.

Arielle gave him a suspicious look.

He stared on at each member one by one and was unsure if he felt sorry for them or not. Like the day spent battling lions in the Coliseum, he felt surrounded. Today would be different, he thought, and he wondered how they would react if one of the lions was suddenly turned on them. "Oh, and one last thing," Pierce said. "You're all fired."

"What? You can't do that," Arielle said. The others began to argue with him.

"Sure I can. Pack up your things and say goodbye."

"You can't fire me."

"The charter says I can. Haven't you read it? You're in charge of

Legal, right?"

Arielle stood up and put a finger on his desk. "My Dad founded these settlements."

"And my grandfather helped design the rockets that got us up here. Or haven't you read about the Steadman rocket? And what did Steven Entner used to say? Oh, yes. On Mars, we may rise and we may fall, but at least we'll be moving forward. I don't think anybody meant for us to drive this place into the ground."

"This isn't over," Arielle snapped as she left the room.

"It is for now. And I think for starters we'll also overhaul the Legal system now that you are no longer overseeing it."

* * *

Later that day, Kyrk and Omar stopped by Pierce's office and sat in the semicircle of chairs in front of his desk. Both looked well-rested and for once it was nice to not face a hostile audience.

"Congratulations on your success," Omar said.

"Congratulations on your success with the Network," Pierce replied.

Omar nodded reluctantly while Kyrk grinned.

Pierce looked at Omar. "So what are you plans now? Are you going to get back into engineering?"

"Maybe if the price is right," Omar said.

"As long as I'm mayor, you'll always have an opening available to you in Network engineering. It's going to take quite an effort to rebuild." He looked over at Kyrk. "And what are your plans?"

Kyrk looked over at Omar and then back at Pierce. "Don't know yet. Ruelle suggested something to me and gave me some books."

Pierce did not see Kyrk walk in with any books and wondered what he meant. "What kind of books? You don't look like the book-reading type."

"I'm not. And I'm having a hard time imagining myself wearing a collar."

"I think the church down the street has an opening. You should check it out," Omar said as he playfully jabbed Kyrk in the shoulder.

"You're not seriously thinking of joining the clergy, are you?" Pierce said.

Kyrk shrugged his shoulders. "Beats talking to streetlights all day."

"Do you think Ruelle would be open to being hired? We have lots of new openings on the City Council. Maybe I should give Neal or Anyk a call. Maybe Neal could take over for Arielle."

"A mathematician in charge of accounting?" Omar said. He shook his head and shuddered.

"If you want I could put a carpenter in charge of Legal," Pierce said.

Kyrk's eyes widened.

Pierce stood up and walked over to the tea-making machine that sat on a counter next to his desk. Since food prices were dropping and production recovering, he finally got around to buying himself a box of tea bags. It was a drink he had not tasted in years. As the machine produced a cup of steaming Earl Grey tea, he gestured toward Kyrk and Omar. "Tea, anyone?"

Chapter Thirty-Five

The city church reopened without fanfare and was led by members of the congregation rather than a formal pastor. They held a well-attended memorial ceremony for Pastor Capshaw with his wife in attendance. As Pierce, Suzanne, and James exited the service they stopped by the video sign out in front of the church. Midori stood there on the sidewalk and stared on at the changing messages on the sign.

As soon as they made eye contact, Pierce spoke up. "Good evening."

"Evening," she said with a slight smile.

He pointed to the sign. "See anything you like?"

She turned away from the sign. "I'm thinking about things."

Tonight she wore a pair of black dress pants and a sharp white blouse. Her beautiful, long black hair was coiled up into a bun. She was not carrying a sword around her waist, but she still was wearing her food badge. Hers, like the others, had long since turned black. Some citizens kept them on despite their obsolescence. It was as if they expected the badges to light up again someday to shine the way into the future or perhaps they were left on to display to the world their owner's proud past.

"I hope you know I ended the badge program," he said.

She looked down and removed the badge as if it was a campaign button for a candidate that just lost a major election. Saying nothing else, she left and went the other way down the street.

"Was it just me or did she seem depressed?" Pierce said to Suzanne.

"She's searching," Suzanne replied.

"For what?"

"Answers."

He stopped a moment and looked up at the church's bell tower. It was not as majestic as the original tower that was destroyed in the Great War, but it was sufficient. Built of rusty Martian brick, it reminded him of a church his mother took him to as a kid.

As they walked on toward Suzanne's house, Pierce said, "I wonder if Kyrk would make a good replacement for Pastor Capshaw."

Suzanne drew back and shook her head. "No."

"Why not?"

"Kyrk was a smuggler. What makes you think he'd make a good pastor?"

"I hear he's reading some books Ruelle Dorner gave him."

"Don't get your hopes up." Her comment was laced with humor.

Up ahead, Midori stopped on the sidewalk and talked with Neal Rexilon. Pierce could tell by the way Neal spoke that something about her captivated him.

"Hey, I was going to offer that guy an accounting job," Pierce said.

"A mathematician? No, Pierce. No." Suzanne shook her head and shuddered.

"Why does everybody say no to that?"

Midori continued to talk to Neal. For the first time in weeks, Pierce saw her laugh and smile. Neal joked around, too, and soon they started walking together down the street.

"Can we get some ice cream?" James asked.

"Ice cream? They haven't had that up here in years," Pierce remarked.

"They have it now. That's where they're going." James pointed excitedly down the street at Neal and Midori. They had walked into a newly opened shop whose sign prominently displayed the words "Ice Cream" in pink and black letters.

"Well, Mr. Steadman, what do you think?" Suzanne said as she gave Pierce a serious look.

"Two scoops of Matterforge cherry nut coming up," Pierce said with a wink.

Chapter Thirty-Six

Pierce sat at home in front of his computer terminal and worked on translating his notebook plans for the city into technical drawings that could be shared via video plate. The process was tedious but as he began to see his old ideas in new ways, a new life was breathed into the drawings. The goal was to have plans for two buildings assembled and ready to present to the City Council at the next board meeting in a week. The City Council itself underwent a tremendous change over the past few weeks with Neal, Anyk, and Ruelle all accepting positions. Omar eventually caved to the idea of working again as a Network software engineer but at an improved pay rate and on terms more to his liking.

He stood up and walked over to his newly rebuilt bookshelf. He pulled out a dusty Earth atlas and reached behind it to grab the felt-lined, burgundy-colored box which contained the ring he bought from Artelius Gray. Although he had given much thought to the setting where he would propose to Suzanne, the timing never seemed right.

He opened the box up to inspect the ring. It was just as beautiful as the day he bought it. He snapped the lid shut when he heard Suzanne approaching. He tucked the box inside of his palm and put his hands behind his back. She entered the room a moment later carrying a large package from the mail carrier.

She eyed him suspiciously and attempted to look around him to see what he was hiding behind his back. "What did you break now?" She said as she stared into his eyes, concerned.

At that he dropped to his knees and took a hold of her right hand. She set the package next to her feet.

"I didn't break anything. Except maybe the bank. But I have something I want to ask you." Before she could react he pulled the box out from behind his back and held it out to her with the lid raised. "There was never a right time for this, so I..."

"Yes," she said without hesitation.

"But I didn't even ask you the question."

Before he could say anything else she took the box out of his hand and kissed him flush on the lips. After he caught his breath, he attempted to put his thoughts back into order. When he stood up, she grabbed a hold of his hand tight enough to cut off its circulation. "When do you think we should tell James?" He said.

She kept her eyes locked on his. "Let's wait until after dinner. Oh, and by the way, this package came in for you. What is it?" She motioned toward the floor.

He looked down and studied the mailing address. "Imported science fiction books."

"More? Where are you going to put them all?"

"That's why I remade the shelves in here. They're bigger now. Remember a few years ago when we stood inside the Magnopolis library? You told me I had to leave all the books behind because you thought they were contaminated."

Suzanne smirked. "So let me guess. Now you're building your own time machine? In your bedroom?"

Pierce pulled her by the hand toward one of the shelves. Just as he did in the library, he reached out and tilted one the books at a forty-five degree angle. "So where do you want to go this time?"

Suzanne stared at the shelves of books and then beamed at Pierce. "How much do you love me?"

Pierce thought about it a moment. "So much I'd go to the ends of the planet for you." Then he thought about what Artelius told him in the jewelry store and he wondered if she was testing him.

"Really?" She said as she led him by the hand back toward the kitchen. At the kitchen table James tinkered with a busybee Pierce picked up off the street. The wings were removed and he had the outer shell of the body split into two halves.

"I was thinking," she continued. "I've wanted to try a new recipe I found." She walked over to the kitchen counter and held up a video plate for him to see. As he got close, she pulled it away before he could read it. "...but I'm a little short on ingredients. Five things to be exact."

"Five things?" Pierce said. On the stove were several pans, including one with boiling water. He wondered why she started in on something with that many missing ingredients.

"I need you to run to the store. Here. Here's my list." She held out the video plate to him.

As he puzzled over the contents of the list, he realized he did not recognize any of the ingredients. "What kind of dish is this? I've never heard of these things. Where would I find a yojofruit anyway?"

She flashed him a thoughtful smile. "They'd have it at the store down the block."

* * *

By the time Pierce arrived at the grocery store, he still had no clue what the items were on the list. He approached the nearest employee he could find and held out the video plate list to her. "Excuse me. Could I get some help finding these ingredients?"

The employee was a woman in her early fifties, with jet black hair and an olive complexion. As she scanned the list, she stifled a laugh.

"What?" He said. "Don't you have those things?"

"Did your friends put you up to this?"

"No. What do you mean? Don't you carry any of these?"

"I've never *heard* of any of these. They all look made up."

"Maybe your manager would know..."

The woman pointed to her name tag. "I am the manager."

Pierce felt his cheeks become flush.

"Who gave you this list?" She said as she put a hand on her hip.

"My wife...I mean my fiancé."

She handed the video plate back to him. "Are you guys getting along okay?"

"We're fine. I mean, I think we're fine. Thanks."

He pocketed the plate and looked toward the store exit. Not wanting to waste a trip or compound his embarrassment, he took one glance at the produce section. A display of bright red apples caught his eye. He picked out five apples and stuffed them into a plastic bag.

After he paid for the apples and left the store, he opened the bag. He pulled out one of the apples and cut it in half horizontally with a pocket knife. It looked normal on the inside with its star-shaped pattern of black seeds. He bit into it and pondered his next move.

Despite all the things he missed from Earth, he could not imagine himself living back there and apart from Suzanne and James. This was going to be his family now and he wanted to do everything in his capacity to make it home. Perhaps in time some scientist would get the terraforming technology right and the three of them could fish in a nice boat on a real lake with the wind at their backs.

* * *

When he arrived back at his house, he passed his hand across the front door entry plate. The door did nothing.

He tried again and still nothing happened. He walked over to the living room window to see Suzanne and James staring at him from the kitchen. They both waved and Suzanne gave him a mischievous grin.

"Ha ha." He said to them through the window glass. "I get it. Five items. But none of them exist. Like the five empty crates. Can you open the door now?"

Again, Suzanne gave him a mischievous, yet loving grin.

"Open the door, Sue. Please. Sue?"

About the Author

Michael Galloway is an outdoors enthusiast whose interests include camping, fishing, hiking, writing, and technology. He has a degree in Journalism, and has been writing software in one language or another for over twenty years. He currently lives in Minnesota with his family.

* * *

Also by Michael Galloway

An Echo Through the Trees
Theft at the Speed of Light
Horizons
Gathering the Wind
Corridors
Fractal Standard Time
Ionotatron